The Phlox
and the Wallflower

A NOVEL

Craig Boroughs

ISBN: 978-0-692-86307-7

This is a work of fiction. Names, characters, businesses, places, events, and incidents are either the products of the author's imagination or used in a fictitious manner. Any resemblance to actual persons, living or dead, or actual events is purely coincidental.

First Printing, 2017.
An e-book edition of this title is also available.

For Whitney

Contents

The Phlox
and the Wallflower

Chapter 1 – Concern for Phlox Adrift

Hannah didn't really how Kelsey ended up on her slippery slope. Adam sure didn't know. Their friends didn't know either. Sure, they knew how Kelsey had been living her life, but they didn't know what she had been battling, internally. All indications were that Kelsey's family had begun to give up hope. Her family got to a point where they only prayed she would make the needed changes.

Kelsey Webb, now twenty-seven years old, grew up in Lubbock, Texas before she moved to the Spruce Creek valley. She attended a four-year college in Texas and while very bright, she left, with only one semester remaining, to follow her boyfriend of that time to Colorado for what was meant to be a temporary break from school to spend one ski season in the Colorado high country. Kelsey had now been in the Spruce Creek valley for over five years.

During the winters, Kelsey worked as a lift operator for the Spruce Creek ski resort, often helping skiers and riders load onto the remaining, older, non-detachable chairlift that required operators to manually pull back each chair to allow riders to load gently. During the summers, she worked part-time on landscaping projects, and while she wasn't the most reliable employee, when she was on project sites, most of the guys on her crew would struggle to keep up with her. She was also such an immediate catalyst to entertain and motivate the rest of the crew that her employer, Drew Erickson, had tolerated much more tardiness and also given way more reprieve to Kelsey's malingering than he ever would from any other worker, but as Kelsey's struggles grew more grim, Drew's patience wore thin.

Hannah Turner dealt with the latest episode from Kelsey on a warm July night. The temperature was forty-eight degrees Fahrenheit, warm by Spruce Creek valley standards where the resort's base area is 8800 feet above mean sea level. Hannah, a thirty-one year old accountant for a gallery in the valley, had difficulty herself identifying her incentive to get involved, but she wasn't showing any indication of giving up. Hannah's introduction to Kelsey and the only previous association she had with her was solely through Hannah's husband's friendship with Drew, but Hannah had become consumed by Kelsey's situation of late and was one of the few remaining soles willing to help. Hannah knew nobody else was helping, which only added to her concern.

Hannah and Adam, Hannah's husband of one year, were living in a modest three-bedroom home down the valley from the Spruce Creek ski resort. Late that Thursday night, Hannah, at five-feet, eight-inches tall, was sitting comfortably, cross-legged, on their bed. The light was on as she gently shook Adam to wake him up. Having just gotten out of bed herself, Hannah was disheveled. Her green eyes were sleepy, her blond hair was slightly tangled, and her dainty feet were clammy, but she still looked as beautiful as ever. Adam had been sound asleep and rightfully so at 1:30 a.m.

"What the hell," he finally groaned, almost inaudibly.

Hannah got up and began getting dressed. "We have to go check on Kelsey."

Adam, lying on his stomach with the left side of his face against his pillow, slowly muttered, "Crazy Kelsey." He turned his head and said, "Hannah, you can't worry about her. She's fine. She's a big girl. She can take care of herself."

"Adam, no, I think she might be in really bad shape this time. Please, let's go." Adam , now thirty-three years old, grabbed his pillow and pulled it around his head and buried his face against the bed. Hannah sighed, slowly walked over to the bed, and gently rubbed his back. "Argh," Adam groaned.

Adam, six feet tall and slim, gradually positioned himself to sit up. Hannah immediately jumped up to continue getting dressed. "Hannah, come here." Hannah, with both her arms in a sweatshirt she was about to pull over her head, let out another deep sigh. She looked at his bleary eyes and purred, "Adam."

"Come here," Adam uttered again, rubbing his eyes. Hannah eased over and sat on the bed. "What's going on?" he asked.

"Adam," Hannah started, beginning to tear up. "I'm so worried about her."

"I know you are. What happened?"

"I don't know," Hannah responded loudly and between gasps, trying to restrain her crying. "Those boys! Why she hangs out with any of them eludes me. They're so mean."

"What happened?"

"I don't know. She called and was crying, telling me how they left her and she had to walk home."

"So she's home now?"

"Yeah, but I really think she might be in bad shape. She hung up on me while she was bawling and now she won't answer the phone or respond to anything."

"Is her roommate there?"

"I don't know, I don't think so. You know her roommate gave up trying to help."

"Hannah, it will be alright. We know she's been through this so many times."

As Hannah looked into Adam's eyes, she slowly whined, "Adam?"

It should be noted that both Hannah and Adam can be acutely selfless and neither of them was anywhere close to resigning to a save yourself lifestyle, so Hannah wasn't surprised when Adam finally replied, "Alright, alright, let me get dressed." As Adam slowly got out of bed with his back to Hannah, he slowly mumbled to himself, "Crazy Kelsey."

Adam was listless and yawning as he put on some blue jeans and an orange, long-sleeved fleece over his t-shirt. He grabbed his favorite Spruce Creek Resort cap to cover his brown hair that was naturally curly, even without the bedhead. As they walked into the living room on the lower level of their three-bedroom house, Cody, their sixty-pound, nine-year-old mutt with thick white fur, continued to lie quietly on the couch. With no expectation that he would be included in the late night activity, Cody didn't raise his head and only watched as they left.

Adam, originally from Ohio, designed trophy homes for a small architectural firm in the valley and had lived in the Spruce Creek valley for nine years. He spent much of the last seven years with Hannah who moved to the valley from North Carolina. Having recently been offered an option to become partner at his firm, Adam was certainly not happy about the distraction on a night before work, but he would do anything for Hannah, as she sure had served that role for him many times.

Adam drove as they progressed up the valley in their German, front-wheel-drive sedan, and being the peak of the summer tourist season in the Colorado high country, they passed a few other cars on the divided four-lane highway, despite the late hour. As they progressed past the main turnoff on the right for the Wallace Gulch valley, Adam kept his focus directly up the road, watching carefully for any elk or other wildlife. The moon was a good three-quarters full, helping to light the surrounding landscape. The moonlight also illuminated the eighteen front-side ski slopes farther up to the right and the high peaks to the left, including Mount Preston, which peaks at over thirteen thousand feet, and the jagged Higgins Peak, that summits at nearly twelve thousand feet.

Hannah, was fidgety as she leaned forward in the passenger seat. They didn't end up spotting any elk but they did see a red fox as they pulled into the parking lot for Kelsey's rental apartment. The fox was certainly wide awake as it moved gracefully and rapidly across the lot, progressing with clear resolve and purpose.

Adam parked, and Hannah hopped out before Adam could turn the engine off. She ran to the front door to Kelsey's first level unit, knocked frenetically, and rocked sideways as she listened for any movement. After a few seconds, she knocked again. Adam strolled up behind her. With still no response, Adam knocked, loudly.

"Come on," Hannah said, pulling on Adam's fleece pullover, and they both stepped into the grass. Hannah led the way, scurrying around the building to the sliding glass door to Kelsey's living room. It was open. "Kelsey," Hannah yelled as they entered. There was no reply. Hannah hurried back to Kelsey's bedroom and then looked in the bathroom. Kelsey was lying still, on her side, on the bathroom floor, with her face against the wall opposite the sink. "Oh Adam," Hannah screamed. "Oh God, oh God, oh God."

As Hannah kneeled down, Kelsey's head slowly turned. "Hannah," she said slowly, sobbing. Hannah exhaled in relief. Hannah sat cross-legged as Kelsey slowly rolled her five-feet nine-inch frame over and rose up to hug Hannah.

"Oh Kelsey, what are you doing on the floor?"

"I was going take a shower," Kelsey stammered, with her smoky voice and subtle drawl. "I guess I didn't make it." Hannah exhaled again in relief as she hugged Kelsey tightly.

Adam stepped in. Peering down at them, he was sure relieved to see that Kelsey was awake and exhibited concern for the first time over the evening's episode. He was used to seeing Kelsey in her tan work pants and loose, rugged, button-down shirts she wears to job sites, but on this occasion, she was still wearing the shorts she wore out that night and the long sleeved sweater that was tight over her full, medium-sized, side-set breasts. The bit of makeup she was wearing was smudged, but with her youthful, tan skin and the natural, auburn highlights glistening in her dark brown hair, she still looked sexy. After a cursory assessment of the situation, Adam cavalierly looked away and moseyed back to the living room.

The living room was an utter mess. Adam paused as he stood, his hands on his hips. He looked around, shaking his head. Adam would never deny his slight obsessive compulsive tendencies, and he began cleaning up. There were dishes on the coffee table, numerous pieces of mail scattered about, shoes and dirty clothes strewn around the room, and multiple ashtrays, each jammed full of cigarette stubs. Adam noticed Kelsey's roommate's cat was lying on the bar between the kitchen and the dining room.

"Wiggles," Adam called as the white and gray American Shorthair calmly watched him, "I don't know how you can put up with this." Adam grabbed as many empty envelopes, mail flyers, and catalogs as he could and stuffed them in the trash. The waste bin appeared full, but he was able to push the garbage down about two-thirds the way.

Hannah, still seated on the cold, tile bathroom floor and holding Kelsey with one arm, managed to reach up to the counter and grab a hand towel. She used it to wipe the smudged makeup from Kelsey's face. "Open your eyes, wide" Hannah whispered as she tossed the towel back up on the counter. Kelsey didn't hesitate, opening her eyelids fully. Kelsey's eyes were bloodshot around her hazel irises, but after Hannah examined her pupils, Hannah sighed in relief and put her arms around her. Hannah noticed goosebumps emerging on her own lithe arms as she held Kelsey close for several seconds. "Adam?" Hannah called, pivoting her head slightly toward the bathroom door.

Adam took a couple steps down the hallway, and in a smart aleck voice, he replied, "Yes, my love."

Hannah gazed down at the dusty, mucked-up bathroom floor and pleasantly asked, "Would you make us some coffee please, if there is any?"

"Yes, my darling," Adam replied in a mocking tone. Hannah rolled her eyes as she looked back at Kelsey. Kelsey and Hannah both chuckled.

"Hannah," Kelsey whispered, "you're so lucky."

Hannah grimaced as she said, "Are you saying you would like to listen to him talk politics all the time?" Kelsey shrugged. "And Kelsey," Hannah added playfully, "I still can't get him to put the toilet seat down."

Kelsey sat up straight and yelled, with a merciless tone, "Adam! Hannah said she's going to leave you if you don't start putting the toilet seat down!" Kelsey screamed even louder, "She'll do it, Adam!" Kelsey grinned, gave a subtle nod, and winked at Hannah as she slouched back into her arms. Adam didn't respond.

After a minute, Hannah whispered, "Come on," as she slowly began to get up. "Let's go see what kind of mess he's making in there."

Hannah and Kelsey moseyed into the living room and sat on the couch. Hannah sat with her back to the kitchen. Kelsey quickly sat beside her and latched back on to her. Adam continued rinsing dirty dishes that were stacked in the sink and on the counter. He loaded the dishwasher as the coffee finished brewing. Despite the noise from the coffee maker and the clanging dishes, Wiggles sat peacefully and watched Adam's every move, seemingly in awe over his effort.

"Your blond hair looks so beautiful in the summer," Kelsey said to Hannah as she pulled her head back and examined Hannah's hair. Kelsey ran her fingers gently through Hannah's hair to loosen a couple tangles. Kelsey looked right into Hannah's green eyes and asked, "Has Adam told you how beautiful your eyes are?"

Hannah pulled her head back and said, "It's been a while."

Kelsey gave Hannah another hug and with a big grin on her face, she peered over at Adam and whispered, "She's so gorgeous."

"Uh, Kelsey," Hannah said, "you stink."

"Well, I was walking down the shoulder of the highway to get home."

"So, where did they go?"

"I don't know. We were down at the Spot. Tyler was deejaying. I was talking to my neighbor, Kyle, and we weren't talking long, but when I turned around, my boys were gone. I hung out, figuring they would be back, but they never came back. I don't know what happened. When the Spot closed, I decided to start walking. Thankfully, Kyle saw me about a half a mile down the highway and gave me a ride home."

Adam blurted out, "Kelsey, cut them off." He smacked the kitchen sink faucet handle to turn the water off. "Hang out with somebody else."

"Oh," Kelsey groaned, "they're fine. They're fun, usually."

"Wolves in sheep's clothing," Adam mumbled. "There not what they seem to be."

Kelsey whipped her head around and snapped back, "I know what wolves in sheep's fur means!"

"Okay, okay," Hannah said, "you need to take a shower. Please go take a shower and we'll find something to eat."

Kelsey wiped her eyes, got up, and plodded toward the bathroom. Her shirt was caught in her shorts, and her strong, slim, tan legs moved rigidly as she trudged down the hallway. Without closing the door, Kelsey turned on the shower. Hannah walked down the hall behind her and closed the door.

As Hannah slowly stepped back into the kitchen, Adam peered over at her. "I know, I know," Hannah whispered. She immediately began to grab dishes and hand them to Adam.

By the time Kelsey finished her shower, Adam and Hannah had about cleaned up the entire kitchen and living room and Adam was clearly comforted by the progress. Hannah had found a frozen pizza in the freezer and had slices heated up and ready for each of them along with some cups of water and a cup of coffee for Kelsey. Kelsey walked out of the bathroom, wrapped in a towel, and after she went into the bedroom, Hannah had to walk behind her and close the bedroom door.

When Kelsey trudged out of her room, her hair was completely wet and she was donning an over-sized t-shirt. She plopped down in a chair at the dining room table and immediately bit into a slice of pizza. Adam was wiping down the kitchen counter as Hannah sat to Kelsey's left and reached over and pulled Kelsey's t-shirt down over her thighs. Hannah watched as Kelsey engulfed her pizza as if she hadn't eaten in days. "Kelsey, you're way too beautiful for this." Kelsey kept her head down and chewed her food.

Hannah put her elbow on the table and rested her head on her hand as she observed the three tattoos on Kelsey's left forearm. Without looking up, Kelsey offered her arm. One of the tattoos was a butterfly with green and yellow highlights that was below a separate tattoo that consisted of a series of stars.

"What does this one with the eagle represent?" Hannah asked as she studied the third tattoo, higher up on her forearm.

Kelsey yanked her arm away. "My brother," she curtly replied.

"They're fine," Hannah said sweetly. "Your artist did a good job." Hannah knew Kelsey also had a large tattoo on her right shoulder blade and two tattoos on the upper part of her right arm, but with the cool weather typical for much of the year in the Spruce Creek valley, all of Kelsey's tattoos were often concealed by her winter clothing. Hannah seemed eager to seize the opportunity to study Kelsey's body art and became particularly interested in the depiction of the bald eagle, which looked regal but pugnacious as it rose out of a portion of the American flag. Kelsey eventually pulled her arm under the table.

After Kelsey devoured the last bite of her pizza, Hannah promptly pushed her slice over. Wiggles, who was still seated in the same spot on the bar, watched Adam as he walked toward the table and sat, opposite Kelsey. "Kelsey," he said, "I'm serious, this is self-destructive behavior. You got to stop cavorting around with those boys and start hanging out with somebody else." Kelsey didn't look up. "Why don't you hang out with Justin?"

Kelsey, with her mouth full, burst out in raucous laughter. "Why don't you hang out with Justin?" she protested.

"It might be great. You don't know. I'm sure he would get you on a better track than you're headed now." Hannah furrowed her brow as she gazed over at Adam.

"Have you ever talked to Justin?" Kelsey asked.

"Yeah, that dude's smart."

Hannah whispered toward Kelsey, "They mostly talk politics."

"No, he's all about the science and technical details behind the issues. He loathes the politics."

Kelsey was rolling her eyes and staring down at the table as she continued eating. Adam slid his slice of pizza over. "Politics," Kelsey slurred, shaking her head. Kelsey suddenly stopped chewing and froze for a couple seconds before she asked, with her mouth half full, "What's going on with that guy anyway? Why is he such a milquetoast."

Adam couldn't help but smile. "He's fine," he replied. "I don't know. So he's admittedly a little timid and a little neurotic."

Kelsey perked her head up and in a mocking, nerdy voice, she said, "The science and technical details." Adam was still smiling which was his first indication of any enjoyment after being abruptly awoken that evening. Kelsey chuckled back and shook her head as she mumbled, "My roommate, Sadie, is always watching that political crap on television."

"Where is Sadie, anyway?" Hannah asked.

"She's at her boyfriend's place."

"Do you feed Wiggles?" Adam asked. "I noticed her litter box is clean."

"Yeah," Kelsey mumbled, looking up at Wiggles who was still wholly focused on Adam. "All that feline does is lie on that counter. She's there when you leave and she's there when you return." Kelsey gazed at Wiggles for a couple seconds and added, "I guess she's a good listener though. We've had some good talks." Kelsey flicked a crumb of pizza crust toward Wiggles but missed. Wiggles didn't budge.

They all sat silently for a few minutes as Kelsey finished eating the last slice of pizza. "Go brush your teeth," Hannah finally said softly. "I'm sorry, but we have to go." As Kelsey went into the bathroom, Hannah found a clean pillow case in the hallway closet, took it into Kelsey's bedroom, and swapped it out with the smelly pillow case on the one pillow on her bed. Hannah also straightened the covers. She piled up Kelsey's dirty clothes that were strewn about the room.

As Kelsey exited the bathroom, she lumbered into bed as Hannah uttered, "Kelsey, you're too beautiful for this." Kelsey hugged Hannah before she lay down. "Hey," Hannah said, "you seriously owe us one."

"Okay," Kelsey mumbled.

"I want you to meet Adam and me at the North Fork tomorrow." Hannah grabbed Kelsey's arm firmly. "Kelsey, I'm serious, you owe us. We're going to talk."

"Okay, okay."

"Okay now, good night, beautiful."

Hannah turned out all the lights, leaving Wiggles in complete darkness, and they locked up the place before heading out the front door. It was a crisp and quiet early Friday morning, and the summer smell of the pines was strong. Adam drove lethargically as they progressed down the shadowy valley. At 3:00 a.m., there were no other cars on the highway and with no wind, it was about as peaceful and tranquil as it gets in the Spruce Creek valley.

"I love you," Hannah said sweetly.

"Okay, but we have to be careful here. We both have to work tomorrow and we simply can't be doing this."

"I know. I know. We'll tell her tomorrow, I promise. Actually Adam, I don't think she's going to make any horrible decisions."

"I guess," Adam said. "I'm actually hoping that's why those boys left her."

Hannah shifted in her seat and asked, "What the heck was that nonsense about Justin?"

"Well, as I said, we can't keep doing this, so I was admittedly looking for an out, but I think it would be great. He needs a friend and I can only assume he would be fine with that friend being a beautiful girl. Also, he might see it as an interesting experiment and enjoy analyzing her overall situation and all the latest complexities of the situation, whatever they are. He may come up with a good approach to help her make the necessary changes."

"One of them could get hurt."

"Maybe, but neither of them would let themselves get hurt too badly."

"You know," Hannah said, chuckling, "Justin may not want to have anything to do with her. I don't think every guy necessarily feels compelled to get together with her."

"I thought of that," Adam agreed. "That might be exactly why he could help her. Maybe that's part of the problem. She has trouble finding anyone she can associate with who doesn't want to go to bed with her ...or who doesn't hate her guts for being so sexy. Hannah, chicks are distracted by it too. It's kind of fascinating. Anyway, maybe Justin won't be so hot and bothered by her."

"Seriously, what's going on with him?"

"Oh, he just likes to hover in the shadows, that's all. He's admittedly a bit faint-hearted and can be reclusive, but that's his comfort zone." Adam shrugged and mumbled, "I don't know. He might benefit more from the deal himself." Adam chortled. "I'm sure Kelsey could get him to talk."

"There is something amiss with that guy, but yeah, if Kelsey can't get it out of him, forget about it." Adam glimpsed over at Hannah and smiled. Hannah looked back up the road and screamed, "Adam!"

A six-hundred pound moose and her two calves were tromping right up the middle of the highway. Adam jerked the steering wheel to the right, their car just narrowly missed one of the calves. He cut the steering wheel back to the left to steer their German sedan back toward the center of the highway, but the shoulder was covered with a thin layer of sand which caused their car to slide. Now sideways, Adam pressed as hard as he could on the brakes, his back pushed firmly against his seat. A deafening screech echoed in the valley as their all-season tires locked up on the dry pavement. As they slid toward the other side of the road, Adam cut the steering wheel again, back to the right, causing the car to cut back toward the center of the highway before finally coming to a stop. They were now facing the opposite direction and their headlights were pointed right at the mama moose and her two calves. The large moose hesitated for a few seconds, snorted, and calmly began moseying farther down the highway. The two horrified calves scampered for a few steps to stay by their mother's side. Adam slowly looked over at Hannah and could see more of the whites in her eyes than he had ever seen in his entire life.

"Did I hit them?" he stammered. "I don't even know."

"I don't think so."

"I'm going to go check."

"No! That mama is still too close. Just go." Adam slowly completed a five point turn to get back facing the right direction. As he proceeded, with brights illuminated, he was now driving thirty miles per hour despite the fifty-five mile per hour speed limit.

Yeah," Hannah said, her voice wavering, "we can't do this anymore. I'm on board. Let's get Justin to talk to her."

Chapter 2 – Wallflower Climate at the North Fork

It was a quiet Friday evening at the North Fork Tavern. With many windows open, the repeated chirps of rufous and broadtail hummingbirds could be heard as they whistled around and fought over the sugar water recently added to two feeders strategically hung in front of the restaurant. A draft from the stiff breeze outside was comforting as the tavern had become warm after the afternoon sun shined through the south facing windows. Summers in the Spruce Creek valley are short, and after being buffeted by an onslaught of repeated cold fronts for months over the winter, summer days are cherished to no end by Spruce Creek locals, especially any mid-July, warm, dry evening.

Only a few patrons were in the restaurant as many residents and visitors were still out enjoying their day at the resort golf course or hiking or biking on the assorted trails throughout the valley. Two families, undoubtedly tourists, were seated at tables and quietly waiting for their food orders. Kelsey's boys were there. With their long hair pulled under their caps and each wearing loose pants and hooded sweatshirts, they were standing at the old wooden bar aligned along the back wall of the tavern. Uncouth as usual, they were yelling at the bartender about all sorts of piddling nonsense as the tavern owner, Jake, stood silently at the end of the bar, monitoring the situation as if he was in full anticipation of having to kick them out at any moment. Four other fellas were seated at the bar and were exasperated by the typical obnoxious behavior from Kelsey's boys, but all long-term locals are used to dealing with such misfits that settle in the Spruce Creek valley after having difficulty finding anywhere else in the country where they could fit in. The regulars were also somewhat more resilient to the presence of Kelsey's boys as it likely meant Kelsey would be arriving soon, and as crazy as she may be, they would certainly hang out for a while in anticipation of getting another opportunity to check her out.

Adam and Hannah were settled next to each other at their favorite high top located between two large windows and opposite the bar. They both arrived from work and were nicely dressed, Adam wearing leather shoes and a thin, white, silk, button-down shirt tucked into his navy, cotton pants. With Adam's obsessive compulsive tendencies, he maintained a consistent, steady rotation through his wardrobe, and his attire on any given day could almost be perfectly predicted by his friends. Hannah was dolled up in hunter green slacks and a loose, light blue blouse. Their backs were to the front door. Cody was tethered to a post and seated, peacefully, right outside the window by their table and could see Hannah's face. Each time Hannah spoke, the sound of her voice would immediately grab Cody's attention.

Josh Carpenter and his fiancée, Emily Barnes, were seated on the other side of their table and were dressed similarly, Josh was wearing a button-down, corduroy shirt hanging loosely over his dark blue jeans and Emily was wearing tan pants and a black blouse that had drawstrings at the end of the short sleeves. Emily was a shift supervisor for the resort hospitality department and Josh owned a photo gallery, Spruce Creek Images, where Hannah also worked. The gallery had been open for over two years now and the business was fully established and doing well.

Emily was twirling the straw in her beverage and was in a slight state of torpor as she gazed with her soft eyes and long lashes toward the Colorado Rockies baseball game broadcast on a large television hung above several old ski run signs on the left side wall. She was somewhat more interested in this particular game since the Rockies were playing the Braves and she had grown up in Atlanta. With long, smooth, black hair, full lips, and puffy cheeks, she had done well to protect her light complexion from the high altitude sun that summer. At five-feet seven inches, Emily was an inch taller than her fiancé, but Josh was stocky and had a shielding presence beside her. While Adam was several inches taller than Josh, Josh was stronger and had always been able to out muscle Adam since they were young, long before the day they both graduated from the same high school in Ohio. Josh also had a pale complexion and would struggle to grow a full beard, but recently, he shaved every day and kept his dry, black hair cut short, per Emily's strict insistence.

Adam and Josh were sharing a pitcher of schwag, light beer while Hannah sipped on glass of ice water. Josh was leaning down on the table with his arms crossed. Adam was also monitoring the baseball game, tuned in on another television hung on the right side wall of the tavern above a pool table and among several large banners and flags for various sports teams from around the country.

"I don't know, Hannah," Josh said, continuing their conversation, "I have to agree with Adam on this one. Kelsey needs to talk to somebody and maybe Justin would have a unique effect."

Emily perked up and rolled her eyes as she asked, "Where are her parents?"

"Texas," Hannah replied.

"Oh," Adam groaned, "she needs to talk to somebody else. Her parents have already worked with her to no avail. That tough love approach probably only made it worse. It's horribly negative and likely part of why she's so down. Plus, they don't remember or understand what it's like to be twenty-seven years old, and they don't have any appreciation for the effect she has on other people, how other people inevitably treat her, and the subsequent impact it all has on the environment around her at any moment. They want to lock her up in their house and force her to get some office job, and no positive effect would come from that." Emily was furrowing her brow as she listened to Adam run on. "They don't appreciate her strengths and weaknesses, and they don't see that she can't apply her strengths trapped in some cube farm."

"Adam," Emily exclaimed, "what do you know about it? Do you really know anything about them?"

Adam shrugged and replied, "Drew's met them a couple times and he got the general pith of the situation."

"Come on," Emily said, "I doubt her boss would be able to pick up on any of that. What really is the problem?" They all looked at Adam, but he threw up his arms and raised his head to watch the television.

"I agree with Adam," Josh said. "Let Justin talk to her."

Emily wriggled in her seat and whispered, "That guy gives me the heebie-jeebies."

Josh lightly smacked her on the arm. "No, no" he said, "stop it. Justin's fine. Look, if he got into some good discussions with her and she was focused on assimilating it all, it would be a fantastic distraction for her. Also, we know he would instinctively work to figure out what's going on with her."

"And how do you plan to get Justin talking?" Emily asked, inciting a chuckle from Josh and Hannah.

"Well, let's see, we could…" Adam started before pausing and pursing his lips. With a slight squint, he looked over at Hannah. She shrugged and shook her head.

Emily was suddenly startled as she nudged Josh firmly and motioned her head toward the door. Adam and Hannah turned and watched as Kelsey arrived, wearing her long, tan work pants and a rugged, plaid, long-sleeved button-down shirt. She strutted over to her boys at the bar and was soon cackling and poking at one of the boys as Jake, still standing at the end of the bar, groaned in anguish before storming back to the kitchen. She was sweaty and dirty but was still the focal point of every patron at the bar. They all became silent, their brains addled over her allure, but Kelsey had long ago become inured of the extensive attention she receives. Adam turned back around and shook his head slowly and rolled his eyes. Hannah, with her right elbow on the table and leaning her head against her hand, kept her eyes locked on Kelsey.

Josh shook his head and looked up at the televised baseball game. "So are the Rockies going to be able to keep this up?" he asked.

"I don't know," Adam responded. "I don't guess anyone could expect their bats to keep bailing out their pathetic pitching." Adam gazed straight ahead at a separate television tuned to the game, and Emily sighed and swirled the straw in her drink. Hannah's head remained fully turned as she stared at Kelsey.

Suddenly, Emily had a grin on her face as she firmly and repeatedly poked Josh. "Would you stop that?" Josh blurted out. "What?" Emily motioned her head toward the door.

Justin, carrying a book, walked in by himself. After stepping inside, he nervously nudged his brown, thick rimmed glasses up on the bridge of his flat nose. His shaggy brown hair bounced as his six feet frame progressed, swiftly and tensely. He always tried his absolute best to not be noticed, but with his signature stiffness, he inevitably created an uneasiness in everyone around him. He complemented his furtive movement with his basic attire, a blue pullover and dark brown pants.

As Justin walked past Adam, Josh, and Emily, he whipped his head toward them, twice, noticing all three of them staring right at him – Hannah was still completely focused on Kelsey. Justin swiveled his head a third time before coming to a standstill next to their table. He squinted his eyes as he looked at Josh and then Adam.

"Hi Justin," Adam said with a smile on his face. "What's up?"

"Uh," Justin slowly uttered in his natural baritone voice, "not much." His eyes were bouncing back-and-forth between Adam, Josh, and Emily.

Josh stuck out his fist to fist-bump Justin. Justin hesitated, grabbed Josh's fist, and shook it. Adam commented in a nerdy voice, "Actually, Justin, the fist bump is more sanitary than the handshake." Justin tilted his head and stared down at the table as he pondered the comment. He then noticed Emily was looking right at him with a big smile. His eyes quickly bounced again between Adam, Josh, and Emily before he rotated his head and pinpointed his favorite table available at the back of the tavern. He lingered for a couple more seconds before rotating his body and walking stealthily toward the small table, nestled between an old wood stove and a foosball table. A large banner with the full baseball schedule for the Colorado Rockies was hung on the wall behind the foosball table.

After Justin sat in a wooden chair at his table, he leaned back, gave one last look toward Adam, Hannah, Josh, and Emily, and kicked his right leg up on his left knee. As he opened his book, a server immediately walked over with a pint of his favorite Colorado microbrew. She brusquely set the beverage on his table, and he politely whispered thanks without raising his head.

"Alright," Emily said, "I see this guy everywhere but I have no idea what he does."

"He works at that non-profit research institute, down the valley," Adam said. "They get small grants to do research on all kinds of stuff. He has a Ph.D. from Iowa State in some natural resources something or other. One of his projects is researching the impact of the black-tusked tussock moth caterpillars."

"What?" Emily responded, furrowing her brow.

"The black-tusked tussock moth caterpillars," Adam replied. "They're invasive and eating needles off fir trees at lower elevations near the Front Range. The trees die and of course thousands of acres of dead trees are bad for the watershed and the water resources and also create a greater risk for wildfire." Emily nodded once as she looked back toward Justin. Adam added, "He does some interesting work."

"Is he rich?" Emily asked, looking back at Adam. Josh spun around toward Emily and glared at her. A look of fury was instantly and deeply ingrained on his face.

"I don't think so," Adam replied.

Emily, completely ignoring Josh, turned again to look at Justin who was sitting peacefully and reading his book. Peals of laughter suddenly emanated from Kelsey and her boys, and Emily turned and gazed toward Kelsey. Emily then looked back at Justin and then looked over at Kelsey again. "I don't know," she droned, "this could have disaster written all over it. Be careful, guys."

"I hear you," Adam said, nodding.

Josh's face still wore an expression of resentment as he peered over at Emily through the corner of his eye. "Is he rich?" he muttered to himself.

Hannah had been staring at Kelsey during Emily's entire questioning about Justin. Finally, Hannah turned her head and looked at Adam. Adam noticed Hannah's eyes were getting glossy. "Oh, Hannah," he mumbled. He leaned over and gave her a light hug and slowly caressed her back. He exhaled deeply and firmly said, "Alright," as he began to get up. "I'll be right back."

Adam walked directly over to Kelsey, who was beaming as she listened to one of her boys cackling and yammering about some piddling nonsense. As Adam stepped up to her, he leaned toward her and uttered something right into her ear. She promptly frowned and turned to look at Hannah. Hannah gave a half-hearted, fleeting wave and immediately looked away.

Adam walked away, continuing briskly toward the restrooms in the back corner of the tavern, behind the wood stove. Kelsey talked with her boys for a few more seconds, but her mood was subdued. After a minute, she plodded over toward Hannah and squeezed herself between Hannah's and Adam's chairs. She gave Hannah a hug.

"What are you doing?" Hannah asked, irritated and with her eyes still glossy.

Kelsey sighed as she pulled back. Her eyes drifted down toward the table. She sat back against Adam's stool. "I know, I know," she mumbled. "It's fine, everything's fine." Hannah turned away and looked up toward the televised baseball game. Kelsey sat on Adam's chair and slowly purred, "Hannah." Hannah shook her head as tears welled up in her eyes.

Josh and Emily quietly monitored the baseball game as Kelsey sat quietly with her head down but still peering up at Hannah. Kelsey never acknowledged Josh's or Emily's presence. When Adam returned, he also took in the televised game as he stood quietly at the end of the table. Kelsey finally let out a deep sigh, slouched in Adam's chair, and gazed down at the floor.

"Kelsey," Adam said. After she peered up at him, he motioned his head in Justin's direction.

Kelsey furrowed her brow, looked in the same general direction, and shook her head, confused. After a few more seconds of looking across the restaurant, she noticed Justin. "Adam, what the hell?" she yelled.

"Kelsey, I cleaned up your apartment. Now you have to do this for me. Go talk to somebody else for a few minutes."

Kelsey looked over at Justin and stared at him with a blank look of wonder. "Adam, why are you trying to foist that nerd off on me?" Hannah sighed in disappointment, and in unison, Adam, Josh, and Emily all gave Kelsey a dirty look. "Ugh," Kelsey grumbled, "what the hell do you expect me to say to that guy?"

Adam pursed his lips and looked up toward the ceiling which had recently been painted during the slow mud season. He then glanced over at Josh. They both looked at each other as if they were trying to telepathically come up with a good discussion topic. After a few seconds, Josh sat up, smiled, and said, "Cap and trade."

Adam hemmed and hawed a bit. He jostled his head and then finally gave a single, firm nod. He looked right at Kelsey and said, "Cap and trade."

"Cap and what?" she yelled.

"Go over there and ask Justin to explain cap and trade to you."

"Adam, I'm not going to do that."

Adam turned toward Hannah. He opened his eyes wide as he stared right into her glossy, bright green eyes. Hannah patted Kelsey on the shoulder. "He did clean up your place," she muttered. "Please just do it. Go talk to him for a few minutes."

Kelsey was maddened as she got up. She began to briskly walk away and shoved Adam firmly against the table, causing the glasses on the table to rattle.

Justin, facing the large television on the back wall that was also tuned to the Rockies game, was slouched with his right leg still resting on his left knee. He had his head down, reading a novel. Kelsey plopped down in one of the chairs at his table. "Alright," she groaned, "explain cap and trade to me."

Justin's eyes got real big as he peered up at Kelsey, his head barely moving away from his book. He slowly sat up, pushed his glasses up on the bridge of his nose, and looked around the restaurant as if he was trying desperately to find any clue to explain the confounding turn of events. "Uh, what?" he faintly asked, letting his long, slim right leg slip off his knee.

Kelsey firmly but politely repeated, "Explain cap and trade to me."

Justin repositioned his bookmark and slowly set the book on the table. He again looked nervously around the tavern. Haltingly, he gazed down at the floor, and with his husky voice trailing off, he asked himself, "Am I in some sort of parallel universe here?"

"I want to learn," Kelsey said convincingly in her raspy voice.

Justin looked right at Kelsey for a couple more seconds. Sweat beaded up on his brow before Josh walked up to him, leaned down, and faintly said, "If someone asks you how to tell time, you don't need to tell them how to make a watch." Josh gave an encouraging, single nod before he proceeded to the restroom.

Justin finally noticed Adam, Hannah, and Emily were all staring right at him and his throat finally loosened. He perked up and gave a nervous swipe to his shaggy brown hair. He scooted his chair under the table and sprightly said, "Okay." Kelsey inhaled deeply, scooted her chair up a couple times, and looked right into his brown eyes. "So you know about global warming, right?"

"Just start from the beginning."

Justin tilted his head slightly. As he looked at Kelsey, he examined her soft lips before noticing her eyes were bloodshot. "Okay," he said, wiggling his head as if to free his mind, "so the air in the earth's atmosphere is comprised of different gases, including nitrogen and oxygen, of course, along with greenhouse gases: water vapor, carbon dioxide, and methane." Kelsey opened her eyes real big as she yawned lightly but continued to look right at him. Justin let his gaze drift blankly off to the side, and his voice was wonky and shaky as he continued, "Greenhouse gases absorb and re-emit radiant energy from the sun along with any feedback radiation from the earth's surface. With increasing amounts of greenhouse gases, more and more of the radiant energy is being absorbed in the atmosphere, and also, more of that absorbed energy is being re-emitted toward the surface of the planet."

"Ugh," Kelsey groaned, whipping her head around to stare at Adam. "You got to be kidding me," she mumbled before she shook her head and slowly turned back toward Justin.

"All the absorbed radiant energy and re-emitted energy," Justin went on, "increases the average temperatures of the oceans and the average temperature in the lower atmosphere."

"Wait, the greenhouse effect," Kelsey blurted out as she sat up.

"Yep, so, the result of the increased amount of greenhouse gases and the increased temperatures has been increased melting of the glaciers and the permafrost and also the sea ice in the Arctic." Justin became distracted as a collective groan emanated from the patrons at the bar after they watched the Braves left fielder tee off for a three-run homer against the Rockies. Justin paused for a few seconds as he watched the replay. The Braves were now up five to four. Justin slowly continued, "Now, there are natural sinks–"

"Sinks?"

"Yeah, natural processes that decrease the amount of greenhouse gases in the atmosphere. But the amount of greenhouse gases in the atmosphere has still gone way up and the increase has been primarily attributed to emissions from human activities since the Industrial Revolution, which started back in the eighteenth century."

Kelsey groaned, "Hold on." She looked over at Adam and yelled, "Adam, I'm going to kill you." Blinking her eyes rapidly, she turned back toward Justin and said, "Okay, the globe is warming due to all the automobiles in the world, the power plants that burn coal, and due to all the forests that were cut down. I already know this. I remember this from school."

Justin was antsy to continue as he shifted in his seat. "Well, …okay, …the forests? That's an interesting component. The forests remove carbon dioxide from the atmosphere during photosynthesis, so any deforestation results in more carbon dioxide being retained in the atmosphere. Also, carbon is released when the forests are burned or debris from any deforestation decomposes."

"Oh Justin, I do love trees so much. You have my attention with that. Whenever I'm working for Drew and I plant a tree, I really do feel like I left a mark on this world."

Justin paused briefly and sweetly said, "That's nice." He shifted in his chair again. "So, as a result of global warming, climate change has been predicted." Kelsey groaned again. She put her right elbow on the table and rested her chin on her hand as she flashed a fake smile at Justin. "With climate change, we'll see increased risk for summertime heat waves and droughts, heavier precipitation, and flooding."

"Yeah, yeah, there's going to be more coastal flooding due to the rising sea level, right?"

"Yeah, from the melting ice in the polar regions."

"So wait a second," Kelsey interjected as she sat up. "The ski resort is nervous about this, right? My neighbor, Kyle, talked to me about this. The resort is of course fearful about any projected change to the snowfall."

Kelsey paused, and as Justin caught Kelsey in thought, he seized the opportunity to take a sip of his beverage. As he took another drink, Kelsey looked down at Justin's right hand, resting on the table, and she reached over with her left hand. Justin became transfixed as he watched her and examined her hand that was tan and dry. She had dirt in her finger nails. His breath hitched as she gently picked up his hand. "Justin, your hands are beautiful," she mumbled. "Wow, you've never worked a hard day in your life, have you?"

"Shoot," Justin retorted.

"I know, I know," Kelsey said, "you're a computer guy or whatever." Kelsey dropped his hand. "So," she said, "we might get more precipitation as a result of global warming and climate change, right? But the weather might be warmer, so we might get more rain but less snow, and the snowmelt might also occur sooner. I know all this."

Justin gritted his teeth and gyrated his head. As he glanced off to the side, he noticed Adam and Hannah were still watching them intently. "Well," Justin droned, "yes, but first, know that there's a difference between the weather and the climate. The climate is the typical weather that might be expected, whereas the weather is simply what is actually experienced at a given time."

Kelsey also looked over at Adam and Hannah and grunted when she saw she was still being watched. She took a deep breath and gently reached over and delicately grabbed Justin's hand again. Justin lightly pulled back but managed to allow his hand to rest in Kelsey's hand. Kelsey responded, "Justin, why are you so shy?"

Justin swallowed, cleared his throat, and said, "So, the weather is what we experienced today, okay? But the climate is what would typically be expected …at a given place …at a given time. The weather may be snowy and cold on a particular day while the typical weather that would be experienced, at that given place, on that day, that is, the climate, may still have shifted to be drier and warmer."

Kelsey let go of his hand. "Alright, I think I got it. So, what's going to happen?"

Justin took another sip of his beverage and leaned back in his chair. He pulled his hand off the table and folded his arms. "Well, it's difficult to predict the severity of future changes to the climate.

We would be remiss to not acknowledge that. But much of the world's population lives in coastal regions that would be directly and significantly impacted. It has been propounded that rising sea levels and any increased occurrence of severe weather could be so substantial that it would result in mass migrations of the world's population, having a devastating impact on the economy and the life of every human being." Kelsey raised her head toward the television, distracting Justin. He turned and watched for a few seconds before continuing, "Assessing such impacts is a bit of a softer science, but it has also been suggested that changes of only a couple degrees could adversely impact the water supply and the ability for societies to produce the food required to fully meet the needs of the world's population."

"Justin, seriously, wrap this up. I sense that you're getting to what can be done?"

Justin smiled. "You asked about cap and trade." Kelsey put her left elbow on the table again and groaned as she dropped her chin into her hand. She opened her eyes, as if she was trying to stay awake, and slowly reached her hand out, but Justin kept his arms folded. "Well," Justin trilled, "cap and trade is a controversial topic." He leaned forward and peered down at her hand, resting on the table with her palm up. He became focused on the tattoos on her arm, specifically the tattoo with the series of stars. "It should probably be emphasized," he went on, "that an overwhelming majority of scientists studying climate change, nearly all scientists for that matter, agree that global warming is already happening and that it will have an impact on the climate. Also, many politicians, including some conservatives, don't refute that the average temperature in the lower atmosphere has been rising, but there are powerful political forces working to discredit any notion that significant climate change is occurring as a result of human activities. I don't want to talk about that. Talk to Adam and Josh about the politics."

"Okay."

"One potential solution, though, is a cap and trade program."

"What's getting capped? What gets traded?"

Justin smiled real big. "Kelsey, what the hell?"

"What?" Kelsey replied, with a scowl on her face.

"Carbon emissions from power plants would be capped, and permits on the amount of carbon that may be emitted would be traded. The permits would be issued by regulators to energy providers and could be traded among power providers. The caps, set for specific facilities, providers, or regions of the country, would be set to decrease over time, to achieve a desired goal of reduced carbon emissions to the atmosphere to ultimately control global warming and alleviate climate change."

Kelsey suddenly let out a deep sigh. She put both her elbows on the table and dropped her head into her hands. "Ugh," she blurted out. Justin sat quietly as he watched her. She then dropped her left arm on the table and lay her head down on her arm, her hand was extended again and hanging over the table, her palm open. "I should go finish school," she murmured.

"What's your major?"

"Botany."

"Shoot Kelsey, you already know this stuff."

"Yeah, kind of, but I didn't know cap and trade was happening?"

"It's not! Well, not on a large scale in America. Some smaller markets have been created and markets have been implemented in some foreign countries, but there is no broad system implemented for the entire United States."

Two patrons at the bar suddenly began to cheer. Justin looked up toward the television and watched a replay. The Rockies right fielder had run at full speed to his left and made a diving catch to end the top of the sixth inning. The bartender subsequently clanged a bell hanging behind the bar, and Justin noticed that one of Kelsey boys had turned and became focused on Kelsey as she sat at his table. Justin looked back and was captivated again by Kelsey's hand, still dangling off the table in front of him. Her fingers were dancing gently. He reached down nervously, gently took her hand, and lifted it back up on the table and held it gently.

"So, how would it work?" Kelsey asked. "Cap and trade in America."

"Energy providers would have caps on carbon emissions," Justin said, tilting his head as he examined her hand further. "Those caps would be reflected by the permits that are issued to them for future emissions. The initial baseline caps would be set to incentivize changes but not punish providers that have regional disadvantages to implementing low emission options. The program also shouldn't punish providers that may have already implemented some low carbon emission alternatives." Justin hesitated as he became transfixed by some rough calluses that were cracked on the back of Kelsey's hand, up from her thumb. The calluses formed a perfect semicircle and matched teeth marks. "With the caps that would decrease slightly over time, companies would be motivated to push energy consumers to use energy more efficiently and providers would also be motivated to meet a greater portion of their future power production needs with zero or low emission renewables: solar, wind, geothermal, hydropower." Justin then yelled, "Kelsey, have you been biting yourself?"

Kelsey jerked her hand away and raised up from the table. "Justin, have you ever seen the wind turbines down near Lubbock?"

"That's a perfect example, right there. Wind turbines are a great renewable option but may not be feasible in other areas of the country. Other regions don't get the sustained strong winds you get down there in Lubbock."

"Ugh," Kelsey mumbled, "I hate the wind, but those massive wind farms are cool."

"For some areas, providers rely on burning coal. Coal is mined from the hills, put on barges, trains, or trucks, and transported to the coal-burning power plants. Under a cap and trade program, coal would still be used, but burning coal emits a high amount carbon, so there would be incentive for providers in these regions to work their best to implement renewable options, and providers in other areas would have an even greater incentive to implement renewables because they could sell their extra permits to utilities that burn more coal. If strict restrictions on emissions were imposed everywhere, some companies would have a tough time meeting the reduced caps, but under cap and trade, they would have the option of purchasing permits for additional emissions above their cap."

Kelsey suddenly reached over and grabbed Justin's beer. She took a big gulp, and Justin's eyes got real big. She swallowed and asked, "You think it could work?"

"Uh," Justin droned, looking at his beer in her hand, "if implemented correctly, sure. It's not a silver bullet solution, but it's a market based system for meeting the goal of decreased carbon emissions, and while it would be more expensive to administer and enforce than a basic carbon tax, it offers much more flexibility and would likely better meet the ultimate goal of reduced emissions versus a cap and tax approach." Kelsey took another gulp from his beer. "Fines for exceeding a cap," Justin continued, with a lump in his throat as he watched Kelsey drink his beer "under cap and trade would, of course, far exceed the cost of permits available on the market. The market would respond to economic forces. During a recession, lower energy demands and lower carbon emissions would result in decreased prices for permits. And, as would be desired during periods of growth, prices would adjust upward with inflation."

"Think cap and trade will happen?"

"I don't know. Now I certainly wouldn't subscribe to any suggestion that we're facing irreversible, runaway climate change, but so many people live in areas that could indeed be so impacted by even small changes to the climate, something should be done now that will deal with this issue for posterity."

Suddenly, one of Kelsey's boys walked up to the table. "Kelsey," he yelled, "what the hell are you doing talking to this drip?" Justin jerked his head up and stared at the boy. Among the sparse stubble on the boy's face, Justin could see his face and neck were slightly pockmarked. He had narrow shoulders and a pooched belly hanging over the waist of his pants.

"Come on," the boy said as he tugged firmly on Kelsey's shirt.

Kelsey got up and started to scurry away, but then stepped back. "I'm sorry," she mumbled. "I should probably go." Justin scoffed and shrugged as he grabbed his book. Kelsey stepped around his table and put her hand on his arm. "Hey, thanks. I'll talk to you later, okay? I'll talk to Adam and Hannah too." Justin, stared blankly at his book and shrugged again. As she skipped back over to her boys, Justin watched her closely.

Adam, Hannah, Josh, and Emily were now shifting in their seats as they watched Justin. "Maybe I should go talk to him," Hannah said.

Josh waved his hand, and Adam added, "He's fine."

"I'll be right back," Hannah said before darting over to Justin's table.

Justin had his book open but was still staring at Kelsey's boys at the bar. As Hannah sat in the same seat Kelsey had used, Justin cleared his throat.

"Uh, Hannah?"

"You alright?"

Justin shrugged. "Hannah, I have a guess as to what's going on here, but what do you expect me to do?

"Just talk to her."

Justin leaned his torso to the side so he could see around Hannah and examine Kelsey. He raised his eyebrows slightly. "Hannah, what happened with her, that night back in January?"

"Ah," Hannah droned as she waved her hand, "don't worry about it."

"Well, I might need to know. I mean, I might need to know what we're dealing with here."

"I'll tell you about it some other time."

"Hannah, she's been biting herself."

"I know. What are you reading?"

"Catcher in the Rye," Justin replied. He chuckled as he added, "I can't relate to this Holden Caulfield guy. I mean, dude, just go back to school."

"Oh, Justin," Hannah said as she shook her head. "You can come join us if you want."

"I'm alright. I have some food coming."

"Okay, well, thanks again for talking to Kelsey. Don't worry about those boys either." Justin shrugged. "Talk to you later," Hannah said as she walked away.

Hannah was smiling real big, showing her bright, white teeth, as she returned toward Adam, Josh, and Emily. As she sat, she whispered, "He's fine." Adam and Josh grinned.

"Oh, guys," Emily said, "please be careful."

"I think we're good," Hannah replied. "I really do."

"You know," Adam started, "we picked the wrong topic. Maybe if we had picked a better topic, she would have told her boy where to go and she would still be sitting there."

"Okay" Josh said, laughing, "what would you have suggested?"

Adam looked up toward the ceiling. After a couple seconds, he blurted out, "Uranium enrichment." Hannah and Emily busted out laughing so loud they attracted attention from one of the families seated near them.

"No, no," Josh said, "how about reinstituting Glass-Steagall, you know, separating commercial banks from investment banks?" Hannah and Emily were rolling their eyes at each other. "No, no, no, wait," he said, excited, as he shifted forward in his seat, "how about labeling for genetically modified foods?"

"GMOs?" Adam said. "No, that's too political. Seriously, you won't get Justin talking politics. He loves talking about the scientific, technical, and analytical aspects of the issues, but he'll clam up when you get to the politics." Adam looked over at Hannah for a second. "I got one," he said, shifting in his seat, "how about the Israeli-Palestinian conflict."

"Oh sure," Josh said sarcastically, "there's nothing political about that. Why don't you just go ahead and have him explain the rift between Sunni Muslims and Shia Muslims." Hannah summarily ceased laughing and was wide-eyed as she stared at Josh.

"Alright, alright," Emily said, "calm down. How do you know you'll even have another opportunity to get them together?"

Adam looked at Hannah, but she shrugged and shook her head. "Hannah," Adam whispered, "seriously, this is good." He reached over to grab her hand. "How could we do this?"

"Hey," Josh said, "let's all go hike Mount Preston on Sunday."

Adam raised his eyebrows and said, "I'm in."

"What's the weather supposed to be like?" Hannah asked. "I seriously doubt we could get Kelsey to join us too early."

"It's supposed to be nice all weekend," Josh said. "We'll go later, and we can assess the situation with the weather further when we get to tree line."

"I gather you want to skip the wine festival?" Emily asked.

"Ah," Josh said, waving his hand, "that festival's nothing but a bunch of drunk old ladies."

"Look, I'm fine with a hike," Emily said, "but are we really going to ask Justin and Kelsey to join us?"

"It'll be perfect," Josh said. "Look, there will be no specific pressure for them to talk. We'll tactfully let them have a moment now and then as it happens. Also, her boys won't be there."

Hannah began to chuckle. "Remember, we're talking about Kelsey. The ice has been broken. She'll probably have her arm around him the entire day, that is, if she shows up."

"Done," Adam said. "Hannah and I will make sure Kelsey's there. We'll also pick up some Knoxville subs for all of us to eat at the peak."

"Yeah," Josh said playfully, high-fiving Adam. "I'll go tell Justin." Josh got up and scampered toward Justin, who was now peacefully eating his signature North Fork Tavern meatball and cheese sandwich. Josh's comments were inaudible as Adam,

Hannah, and Emily watched quietly. Justin shrugged before finally nodding. As Josh ran back to the table, he said, "He's in. Emily and I will pick him up at his place Sunday morning. Hannah, you're right. He does have a bit of a glow to him that I don't recall seeing before."

"Ugh," Emily groaned, "guys, please keep your bearings on a healthy objective." Josh put his arm around Emily's shoulders.

They all enjoyed the rest of their evening at the tavern, pigging out on six appetizers. They watched the Rockies ultimately lose their game to the Braves by a score of eleven to nine. While they were paying their check, Justin was walking out and stopped by their table. "Dang bullpen," he muttered to Adam.

Adam groaned before Josh replied, "It will be their doom again this year."

"Well," Justin said with a smile, "I guess I'll see you Sunday morning."

"Mount Preston beckons," Josh exclaimed.

"See you Sunday, Justin," Hannah said. After he departed, she laughed. "Oh my goodness, he's so happy."

Emily closed her eyes and smacked the palm of her hand against her forehead.

Chapter 3 – Adaptation and Resilience on the Links

Drew stood calmly, looking east down the fairway of the fifth hole at the Spruce Creek golf course, visualizing his tee shot as the daylight gleamed off the pond to the left. Behind the tee, leaves rustled on several aspen from the strong left-to-right breeze. Drew, sturdy, tan, and handsome with a strong face, had brown hair cut so short it was unaffected by the wind. Donning a light blue polo and dark brown, synthetic golf pants, Drew stepped forward, exuding his typical confidence as he squared his two hundred pound, six-feet two-inch frame perfectly for the line for his drive. With his knees soft, he secured his interlocking grip and exhaled as he slowly rotated his head toward the fairway one last time to survey the line for his shot.

Adam, wearing long, cotton pants along with a black fleece vest over a white, knit polo, was standing back to the right with his hands resting on the end of his driver that was balanced perpendicular to the ground. Down a rocky slope to the left, two elderly gentlemen and a lady were putting on the fourth green while unbeknownst to them, two ravens had alighted on their golf cart, opened the zipper pockets to their golf bags, and begun scrounging around for an afternoon snack.

Methodically, Drew breathed in slightly as he slowly began his back swing, rotating his hips and transferring his weight to his back foot, and then, with his left arm straight, his wrist cocked, and his back facing the fairway, he quickly initiated his downswing. As his club descended, he rotated his shoulders back even with his line and released his wrists as he squarely impacted his ball. With his head still down, he listened to the perfect ping sound as his club impacted his ball. The ping echoed off the bluffs to the south as he watched his tee flick backwards, the tee rotating in the air while he finished his follow through. His hips turned toward the fairway and he gradually looked up with his shoulders swiveling toward his shot. His weight now transferred to his front foot and his driver now static behind his head, he watched as his ball soared out over the pond to the left.

"Come back," Adam whispered.

As the ball continued to ascend, it gradually sliced back over the fairway and then began to drop, finally hitting on the left side of the fairway and skipping three times before rolling several more yards, coming to a stop in the middle of the perfectly cut Kentucky bluegrass. Drew relaxed his stance before he reached down to grab his tee and took a couple steps back. He was now set up with a perfect line to the green for his second shot.

"Dang," Adam whispered. "Good ball," he added louder with inflection to his voice as he advanced to the tee box.

Exactly halfway between the two white markers, Adam placed his yellow wooden tee in the ground. His tee had Spruce Creek Golf Resort written in tiny letters along the shaft. He perched one of his orange, used golf balls on the tee and stepped back to complete two practice swings. He shook his head with uncertainty as he stepped forward and lined up for his drive. With a slight exhale, he slowly completed his backswing and quickly executed a downswing through his ball. The ping sounded nice and the drive lofted straight down the middle of the fairway, at first, but then hooked hard to the left. Adam and Drew watched as the ball kept hooking and hooking before eventually splashing twenty feet out in the pond. The loud plop scared three ducks that had previously been paddling peacefully on that beautiful Saturday afternoon. Adam stood still, holding his follow through for several seconds before he finally let the head of his club drop to the ground. He peered back at Drew.

Drew smiled and wiggled his eyebrows. "Take a mulligan," he said.

"No," Adam groaned as he searched for his broken tee. "I'll drop at the drop zone." They slowly strolled over to the golf cart and put their drivers in their bags. As they sat down, Adam asked, "How can I be so bad at this game yet still be having so much fun?" Drew shrugged and stomped on the accelerator. The cart jerked forward, and they motored up the path to the drop zone where Adam subsequently smacked a fairly solid shot with his five iron. His ball rolled up close to where Drew's ball lay. They eased up to their balls and got out slowly, for they were going to have to wait a few minutes for the foursome in front of them to finish putting.

"So," Drew said, "what the heck were you and your wife up to last night at the North Fork with Ms. Webb and Mr. Hayes?"

Adam furrowed his brow as he looked at Drew. "How did you hear about that?"

Drew took a step to the side and commenced setting up a practice line for his next shot. "Oh," he said, "a couple of my crew members were there and they were trying to figure out why Ms. Webb would be talking to that guy. They told me about it this morning."

"Did Kelsey work this morning?"

"Yeah," Drew said. "She showed up. All the other guys were giving her a hard time for talking to Hayes, but she actually defended him, resolutely."

"I don't know," Adam mumbled. "We'll see. I may be wrong, but I think it might help her get on a better path."

Drew rolled his eyes. "What the heck would she talk about with that guy?"

Adam smacked his lips and replied, "Cap and trade."

"What?" Drew said, as he busted out laughing.

Adam chortled as he dropped his head. "It was great," Adam said, still chuckling. "I'll give her credit, she hung in there for a while."

"Oh, man," Drew scoffed, "was Mr. Carpenter there?"

"Yes, Josh was there."

"I could have figured. It sounds like some scheme he would work up to push his agenda on somebody else and try to turn her into one of your bleeding heart liberals."

"No, no," Adam said, "Justin's not political. He's all about the science."

"Shoot," Drew groaned. "Cap and trade? Are you serious?" Adam shrugged. Drew kept shaking his head as he stood quietly, watching the foursome move about the green. Adam looked off in the distance to the south. A line of three mountain bikers was progressing up a single track on the hillside at the edge of the golf course. "Were her dumbass boys there last night?"

"Yeah," Adam groaned as he slowly shook his head. "Hey, Hannah's really hoping you'll keep her on with your landscaping crew for a while longer. I think I may have Hannah convinced that this Justin approach will work. We're all going to hike Mount Preston tomorrow."

"I'm too busy to let anyone go at this point in the season. Plus, when Ms. Webb actually shows up, she's much better to have than the ineptitude I have with the rest of my crew, but your wife needs to understand that I'm running a business. It's not some charity organization. I don't want to have anything to do with that path she's headed down, and when she doesn't show up, I'm the one caught in the lurch with a missing crew member." Adam looked at Drew and gave a firm, acknowledging nod.

They stood quietly for several seconds. Drew's mind wandered and Adam looked to the north at Mount Preston. Two adjacent avalanche chutes, off to the west of the peak, were naturally shaped by the cleared trees to almost perfectly look like a large S and a large C, which serendipitously worked well to signify the arrival at Spruce Creek for anyone driving up the valley. At that point in July, little snow was apparent above tree line, and Adam confirmed that they would be able to count on the trail being clear and dry all the way to the peak.

"Crazy Kelsey," Drew mumbled, gaining Adam's attention. Drew shook his head and then froze. "Boy," Drew stated, "she sure is sexy though, isn't she?"

Adam raised his eyebrows. A serious look fell over his face as he firmly said, "Yes, she is."

"It does break your heart a little."

"What's that?"

"She's so smoking hot, but that commodity will fade someday. If she continues down this path, she'll be set up with nothing. She still has an opportunity to set herself up with a beautiful future, but she's squandering it away." Adam shook his head and stepped up toward his lie as the foursome in front of them began to lumber off the green. "No, but Adam, you should see what she looks like in a hard hat." Adam smiled as he took a couple practice swings. "I would have loved to have seen the expression on Hayes' face when she walked over and plopped down at his table last night."

They focused intently on their golf game as they played out the fifth hole and carried on with their round. Drew was the better golfer, but since they were starting each hole from the white tee boxes, Adam was hanging in there, only down by six strokes when they reached the par-3 eighth hole. The foursome ahead of them was still waiting to tee off as Drew and Adam sat in their golf cart, parked at the top of a rise along the path, about thirty feet back from the tee box. A girl driving a beverage cart had finished serving snacks and cocktails to the foursome and eased by to make sure Drew and Adam were fine, though she knew they never ordered anything. As she drove away, Drew angled his head to ogle her thin, tan legs. Drew then wiggled his eyebrows at Adam.

As they sat quietly, a stiff breeze picked up, annoying the first golfer ahead of them as she lined up her tee shot. "So," Drew whispered, "how did Mr. Hayes articulate cap and trade without getting into the politics?"

"He addressed the background science behind global warming and climate change and how a cap and trade program could work if ever implemented."

"Shoot," Drew groaned, "Adam, it's all a bunch of hokum. You haven't been suckered into that apocryphal nonsense, have you?"

"Oh, come on," Adam said, "are you going to start regurgitating what your radical, conservative commentators expound on your a.m. radio and your twenty-four new channel? Drew, they're all being paid indirectly, if not directly, by the big energy companies to specifically brainwash American voters into letting them continue to burn as much of the country's fossil fuels as they can–"

"Oh my gosh," Drew interrupted as he jumped out of the cart and started rummaging through balls in his golf bag.

"They got you hoodwinked," Adam went on , "all so they can maintain their extravagant lifestyles at the expense of our planet where your children and your children's children are going to live for decades." Adam kept a straight face but then cracked a smirk as he looked back at Drew. "You aren't going to pop me, are you?"

"You're the one that's all brainwashed with this bunkum. Adam, you can't place any credence to that apocryphal nonsense. Any changes evident in the data are simply due to the natural variations of the earth's axis of rotation and the orbit around the sun along with the solar output and volcanoes. Check the satellite data."

"And there it is," Adam blurted out, laughing. "Satellites? You Pavlovian dog! All you can do is regurgitate what some talking head said to you on your twenty-four-hour news channel. Maybe you should focus on the temperature data from the measurements at the earth's surface. Anyway, there is no evidence from the satellite data of any increase in solar irradiance over the past few decades that would explain the temperature increases measured in the lower atmosphere, and if there was an increase due to solar irradiance, temperatures in the upper atmosphere would be warming too, but the warming has been confined to the lower atmosphere. Check your facts, why don't you?" Adam pulled the left collar of his shirt up over his nose as he cracked another uncontrollable smile.

"Oh, the scientists are just trying to protect their research funding. Heck, I bet that lecture, your boy, Hayes, gave Ms. Webb last night was probably the identical specious, spurious spiel he keeps repeating to keep his research funds flowing." Adam couldn't help but laugh at Drew's well-timed alliteration. "Look Turner," Drew continued you can't wreck the entire country's economy or the entire world's economy over some rubbish trumped up by a bunch of tree huggers."

A couple of the golfers ahead of them turned and stared at Drew. Drew sat down in the cart as Adam took a big gulp of water from a bottle he had in the cart cup holder. "I understand the impacts are hard to predict," Adam said in a hushed tone, "but average temperatures have suddenly spiked at rates that do not conform to anything close to what would be expected based on natural variations from the past few thousand years. Arctic ice is melting and glaciers are retreating at an alarming rate. There is already evidence of changes that serve as a harbinger of what's to come. A rise in the sea level is already apparent. Extreme weather events are all too apparent and can be so devastating." Drew was shaking his head and rolling his eyes. "The only way scientists have been able to simulate the recent changes with calibrated and validated computer models is by including the added human induced emissions of greenhouse gases."

"Why don't you calibrate and validate this?" Drew said as he leaned over and ripped a rumbling fart in the direction of Adam.

"Well, that's the problem right there," Adam exclaimed as he pushed Drew firmly. Drew giggled childishly. "It's your own personal methane emissions," Adam yelled, "causing the increase in greenhouse gases in our atmosphere." The four golfers at the tee all turned around again and stared as Adam and Drew subsequently tried to stifle their laughter. Thankfully, the wind was brisk enough that the stench from Drew's flatulence wafted away. "It's because of you and all those flatulent cows," Adam went on, "trying to keep our meat eater appetites satisfied, out there farting and burping mass amounts of methane into our atmosphere." Adam started giggling and was having trouble getting out his next comment. He was poking Drew as he whispered, "Hey Drew," continuing to giggle uncontrollably, "Justin told me once that not all humans produce methane."

Drew was shaking his head as he smiled. "Did he conduct any experiment to reach this conclusion?"

Adam stammered, "I wonder if he put together a representative sample of subjects and had them all try to light their farts to come up with a percentage of humans that produce methane." Drew was shaking his head as he giggled. "I'm telling you," Adam added, "somebody studied it."

"Did the government pay for these studies?"

The wind had finally eased up, and Adam and Drew became quiet as they watched the last two golfers in front of them complete their tee shots. The foursome then hopped in their carts and motored down the path to the green. When Drew subsequently hit the accelerator on the cart, his golf bag flew off the back of the cart. His clubs clanged as they landed on the cart path. Adam had his shirt pulled over his mouth yet again and was laughing over the success of his little jape. He had loosened the cart strap around Drew's bag.

"You nincompoop," Drew rebuked with a sneer. He shook his head as he got out to replace the bag on the cart. He punched Adam firmly as he sat back down. As soon as he punched the accelerator, Adam's golf bag flew off the back of the cart and clanged on the path. Drew blithely drove on down to the eighth tee box.

As Adam walked back up to get his bag, Drew grabbed his rangefinder off the dash, stood up, and looked through the eye of his scope toward the green. "One-seventy-three to the pin," he mumbled as Adam slogged back toward the cart with his clubs.

"I hope I'll be good enough someday that it will matter for me to know distances," Adam said, strapping his bag back to the cart. "Drew, someday, I'll be able to hit predictable distances with each club. I will."

"You're getting there."

"Is your scope using GPS data?"

"No, it sends a laser pulse down to the prisms on the pin and determines the distance based on the time for the laser to bounce back."

"Cool."

"But yeah, you can download course data to use with GPS devices."

They both slowly grabbed clubs out of their bags. Drew selected an eight-iron and Adam picked a six-iron before they strolled out to the tee markers, took a few practice swings, and assessed their southerly line toward the green. As they waited for the foursome in front of them, Adam became focused on one of the trophy homes, located about a fifty yards to the left of the tee.

"Did you design that one?" Drew asked.

"No, my boss, Ken, designed that one before my time."

"I'm telling you, Turner, you need to go out on your own."

Adam sighed and shook his head as he looked up and noticed a flock of about twenty Canadian geese, flying directly overhead in a perfect V pattern except for one lone straggler at the edge, having difficulty catching up and getting into formation.

"Adaptation and resilience," Drew suddenly blurted out as he slowly swung his club with one hand. Adam, still watching the geese overhead, hemmed and hawed a bit. "Humans are amazingly capable to adapt to a changing environment," Drew went on. "If people are living in an area susceptible to extreme weather events, they can move. They can irrigate to better meet their food needs or grow different crops."

"Well," Adam said, pulling his six iron around his back and up onto his shoulders, parallel to the ground, "whether adaptation can work will depend on the specific impact being addressed.

Effects around the globe will vary tremendously. Coping strategies for some impacts may be efficient and easy to implement; whereas, strategies to deal with other impacts may not be feasible at all." Adam looked down as three weasels had wandered out of some burrows near the tee box. "Also," he went on, "some affected areas simply won't have the resources to implement such strategies. The cost to deal with the impacts after the fact might be much greater than the upfront costs to avoid or at least alleviate the impacts." Adam stared at the three weasels, moving about anxiously. "Hey," he whispered whimsically, "that weasel on the left looks like a golden ferret. You know, I'd like to see you use your sand wedge and hit a golden ferret today. What do you think about that?" Adam slowly dropped his six iron to the ground, causing all the weasels to scatter back to their burrows. "Ah, I guess it would be a miracle to see a golden ferret, eh?"

"Take the hit," Drew exclaimed.

"What?"

"Human beings are so resilient. People have been knocked down so many times by wars, famine, the plague. So we may be dealing with some climate change. People just need to gird their loins."

"Gird their loins?" Adam asked as he started to laugh. "People don't want to gird their loins. Plus, many people that might be greatly affected are less fortunate people in less developed countries and also the ones that have had the least impact on global warming. And again, there would be costs for communities, local governments, and private entities to modify infrastructure, set up critical services, and establish other resilience strategies. Drew, if it could all be avoided or the effects could be significantly alleviated–"

"Oh," Drew groaned, "the impacts of cap and trade, or whatever so called solution, would be so much more damaging than the effects of any slight change to temperatures."

"Efforts to reduce depletions to the ozone layer worked and that didn't wreck the economy. Even if cap and trade is off the table, please acknowledge that there are other options, improving energy efficiency, reforestation, and certainly, low carbon emission energy sources, renewables." With an expressionless face, Drew farted in Adam's direction again. Adam noticed the foursome in front of them placing the flagstick in the cup and hastening off the green. "Alright," Adam said, "show me how it's done."

Drew was quick with his preparation and promptly smacked a high, arching drive with his eight iron. His ball landed pin high but was off to the right of the green and kicked to the side into the rough. "Argh," Drew shouted. "See what you did?" Drew picked up his broken tee and threw it off to the side. "Prattling on with this cap and trade gibberish. That was your fault."

Adam snickered as he placed a yellow, used ball on the grass within the tee box. "Maybe I've discovered the kryptonite to bring down your game. I merely need to talk climate change." Adam lined up his shot and hurriedly completed his swing, punching the ball more than hitting it, but his ball carried over the dense rough, bounced on the front fringe, and rolled on the green, nearly hitting the pin before rolling farther and stopping on the back fringe. "I don't guess that was pretty, but I'll take it."

Drew and Adam progressed with their round. They of course continued to razz each other along the way. Drew's game was assuredly more affected by all of Adam's banter, but Drew still maintained a sizable lead on the scorecard. The foursome in front of them had not impeded their progress again until they reached the par-three sixteenth. Facing east, the sun was now behind them and the rays were reflecting off a cascade of water gurgling over some rocks in a ditch that passed, right to left, in front of the tee box. Thick wetland vegetation surrounded the stream, leaving few other playable options for a tee shot unless the ball landed on or around the green. The pin was one hundred and eighty-six yards from the white tee box and the cup was located center-left on the large circular green that gently sloped right to left. The green was surrounded by a narrow rim of cut grass and three bunkers with one bunker in front to the right and two bunkers to the left. As they sat quietly in the cart, parked next to the tee box, Drew's was still miffed over the downturn in his game through the back nine.

"Drew," Adam said, "melting ice is irreversible. We won't be able to take a mulligan."

With perfect timing, Drew leaned to his left and emitted another resounding fart in Adam's direction. As Adam shook his head, Drew said, "Turner, if I'm going to be a part of this, you seriously need to get Mr. Hayes and Ms. Webb talking about something else. If he gets her all brainwashed with this climate change drivel, I'll have to have to follow-up and work with her to disabuse her of this nonsensical, trumped-up hoax that those science people won't let go."

"Alright, alright" Adam replied. "We will. I promise."

Drew wiggled around in his seat in discomfort. With a grimace on his face, he grunted, "I really need to go talk to a man about a horse."

Adam dropped his head as he chuckled. "Three more holes to go. Are you going to make it?"

"I don't know."

"Alright, another topic. Here are our ideas so far: uranium enrichment, Sunnis versus Shias, the Israeli-Palestinian conflict." Drew rolled his eyes. "I'm telling you," Adam added, "it will be fine. Justin doesn't have a political bent. He detests politics. His interest is solely in the science and the facts of a situation. He wants to see decisions made based on proper analyses of the details related to each issue. It will be good to get him talking about this stuff."

Drew nudged Adam lightly and motioned his head up to the sky. A large red-tailed hawk was flying off to their left. The white underbelly could be seen plainly against the dark blue sky as it soared with its broad wings holding fixed. As it surveyed the landscape below, it tilted to the right, showing the light brown plumage on its back and its wings followed by its dark red tail.

"Okay," Adam said as they both watched the hawk glide off to their right, "what would you have Justin talk about?"

Drew thought for a moment and then sat up in his seat, his mood becoming lighter. "The gold standard. Yes, get your little madcap, Hayes, to expound the gold standard to Ms. Webb."

Adam nodded and firmly said, "Okay, you got it. Actually, we're going to get Kelsey to ask him about uranium enrichment tomorrow, but we'll file that one away. The gold standard. I like it."

"I still don't understand, though. What do you figure is going to happen?"

"With what?"

"Ms. Webb."

"Oh," Adam droned as he slouched slightly in his seat, "I don't know. As it stands now, Kelsey's obviously gotten into a bad rut with those toxic, virulent boys and that's all she knows. It's the only place where she's comfortable, and when she's not all messed up with them, she falls into a horrible funk. I'm hoping that by talking to Justin, it will help her visualize a whole big world that's out there and the many other directions she can take with her life. She can still make her life extraordinary. She can further her education, by whatever means she likes, and develop a path to rewarding, meaningful work that will allow her to prosper financially. She can develop new relationships and friendships with people that will respect her and love her. I'm hoping Justin will help her see that she can live healthy, in every way, and be so happy from taking different approaches to life, as opposed to finding happiness through other means."

"I'm sorry for being pessimistic, but I've resolved that it would be a miracle if anyone could get her sorted out at this point. What about Mr. Hayes?"

Adam smiled. "Well, yes, it is interesting to think how it might all have a bigger impact on him."

"I have no idea what's going on with that guy," Drew uttered. The foursome in front of them began moving off the sixteenth green, and Adam and Drew climbed out of their cart and grabbed clubs from their bags. With his nine iron, Drew hit a beautiful, lofting tee shot but it landed in the right bunker. "This is all your fault," Drew mumbled. Adam hastily and softly punched his seven iron, and his orange ball barely cleared the wetlands, but bounced past the first cut and rolled to the front fringe.

After settling into the cart, Drew stomped on the accelerator and zipped down the path to the green where he slammed the parking break, hopped out, yanked his putter and sand wedge from his bag, and walked briskly toward the right bunker. After moving past Adam's ball, Drew dropped his putter and stepped into the bunker. Approaching his ball, he exhaled deeply, assessed the line for his shot, and then got set in the bunker with a wide open stance. He twisted his feet a few times to dig his shoes into the sand and took several seconds to regain his composure. Adam stood motionless beside his ball as he watched patiently. Drew pulled his sand wedge back and took a full swing through his ball. A large plume of sand exploded out of the bunker as Drew's ball rose up, seeming to float in the cloud of sand. The ball landed ten feet on the green and began to roll smoothly and steadily toward the hole. The green was fast and as the ball kept rolling, Adam began to cheer. Drew scurried out of the bunker and stepped up to the fringe to get a better view of his ball. The ball continued to roll but gradually slowed down as it veered, right to left, directly toward the hole. The ball maintained just enough momentum to reach the hole and …plop in.

"Are you kidding me?" Adam yelled. "A golden ferret!" Adam stood, mystified. "Wow," he whispered, "I guess miracles can happen. You did it. You just hit a golden ferret."

They finished their round with Drew shooting an eighty-four and Adam ending with a ninety-eight. Adam was elated to finish with a score under a hundred.

Chapter 4 – Fissile on Mount Preston

Cody, untethered, was galloping in front as Josh, Adam, Kelsey, Hannah, Emily, and Justin continued their trek up to the peak of Mount Preston, located on the north ridge down the valley from the Spruce Creek ski resort. Adam, with his brand new, leather hiking boots, synthetic long pants, t-shirt, and light blue backpack, proceeded with his head down and his eyes locked on Josh's worn hiking boots and the tattered heels on Josh's old, blue jeans. Josh was carrying a light daypack and wore his typical hiking attire that also comprised of a cotton t-shirt with a stretched neck and a full-brimmed, tan hat. Kelsey, donning the clothes she wears regularly to her landscaping job, was a few steps behind and trifling about the latest celebrity gossip while Hannah and Emily responded to Kelsey's tidbits with repeated laughter. Hannah and Emily were moving steadily in their tight, three-quarter sleeved, workout shirts, lightweight hiking shoes, and matching black hiking pants. Justin, lumbering along in the back with his hands grasped tightly to the straps on his black backpack, wore an old pair of dress slacks and an Iowa State cotton t-shirt. He huffed and puffed most intensely, and his shaggy, brown hair was already drenched with sweat and flat on his head. His spectacles were mucked from the sweat dropping off his brow.

The hike began with a steady one-mile ascent on a well-trodden path through the dense forest of thin lodgepole pine trees, most of which were dead as a result of the pine beetle epidemic. They reached a grassy, open area that was afforded with abundant sunshine that Sunday, and as they kicked through long grasses, thistles, and various wildflowers, Carolina grasshoppers would occasionally take flight, flitting their wings and creating their signature, loud crepitation sound that was so common it didn't have a startling effect on any of them. To their right, the east end of the Spruce Creek valley was in clear view, and Higgins Peak towered up to the northeast. About forty ravens could be seen flying high over the valley, and only a faint hum could be heard from the din of highway traffic below.

As Kelsey kept jabbering, Josh interrupted her, "How would you like it if people gossiped about you the same way you talk about all these celebrities?"

"Oh," Kelsey retorted, "they can take it. They're all so bright and rich, they deserve it. It seems natural for all the customers of their industry to want to lock on to anything negative they can find. It goes with the job. We still adore them for being so talented and beautiful." Josh shook his head as Kelsey loudly said, "Anyway," and recommenced with her latest story.

It was a warm day with little wind and the bugs were out. The bug season only lasts a few weeks at that elevation in the Spruce Creek valley, but a few mosquitoes managed to home in on their exhaled carbon dioxide, identifying them as prime targets before launching their attacks. Emily cursed to herself as several horseflies were particularly interested in her. They knew there would be fewer bugs up higher.

As they reached a slight incline in the trail, conversation waned and they all focused on maintaining a steady breathing rate for several minutes as they motored smoothly up the steeper slope. With the newfound silence, they could hear Porcupine Creek babbling a hundred feet off to the right. The snowmelt runoff had receded, so the flow in the stream was down, but the sound of water moving rapidly down the creek was soothing nonetheless. Through the trees, they could see a well-used, level campsite by the creek that included a maintained fire ring.

Cody was visibly disappointed by the slower pace and scurried off the trail to assess the sources for the endless number of scents. As the trail leveled out, they entered a dense, stand of mature aspen. Getting his breath back, Josh said, "There have been reports of bears harassing hikers up here this summer."

"Josh!" Emily screamed.

"Oh," Josh said, "no bear is going to want to have anything to do with us, and we're most certainly making enough noise that we won't surprise any animal today."

"Cody will protect us," Hannah said.

"Oh Hannah," Kelsey purred, "the state parks and wildlife department had to euthanize a sow and her cub last week. They were getting in dumpsters, but after they entered one of the homes up on Pika Court, that was it." The others had read the story in the Spruce Creek News and were mumbling in acknowledgment and shared grief.

Adam and Josh started talking about football, and as they took control of the conversation, Emily groaned in discomfort. As the discussion persisted, Hannah genuinely tried to participate. Justin continued to lumber along silently in the back, his head down, his breathing more labored. He seemed to be in a groove and content so nobody said anything to him.

Two and a half miles up the trail, they crossed Porcupine Creek at a crossing that can be particularly awkward, even after the runoff, but they were able to hop among several strategically placed logs and stones to cross without getting their shoes wet. After progressing up a gradual ascent for another three quarters of a mile, they reached Conrad's Cabin. There's not much to the cabin anymore, only remnants remain from the area that bustled in the late nineteenth century. They stopped to hydrate and Adam and Josh were soon yakking, jeering, and gibing each other. Hannah checked on Justin, who had remained speechless, but he assured Hannah he was fine. She felt better when he started pointing out some dwarf mistletoe on branches of the lodgepole pines around them. Dwarf mistletoe is a leafless, parasitic plant that grows on branches of lodgepole pines throughout the forest, causing growth loss and increased tree mortality.

The trail heading up from Conrad's Cabin was much steeper, and after restarting, they were all immediately gasping for oxygen and became quiet, except for Kelsey who had begun singing a song to herself that nobody recognized. Even Cody was panting as he walked in front, his head down, right in line with the trail. While Josh wasn't breathing as heavily as Adam, he was sweating profusely and his hair was soaked.

They hiked up the steeper pitch for half an hour and each was breathing heavily. Justin had fallen back about hundred feet but was still within view. "Hey," Adam said to Josh, "I'll race you some other time but maybe we should stop at that opening in the pines at the third switchback and let Justin catch up."

"Sure," Josh said. Josh instantly picked up the pace for their final sprint to their new defined stopping point. Adam groaned, shook his head, and skipped a couple times to regain his position on Josh's heels.

It only took Josh and Adam a few minutes to reach the stopping point which afforded a beautiful view to the southwest. Kelsey, Hannah, and Emily strolled up shortly thereafter. Josh sat, cross-legged, over a thin bed of pine needles and petted Cody. Adam stood, peering through the trees toward the northwest at a large wildlife refuge and a portion of Lake Labash that was barely in view farther down the valley. As Hannah eased up to Adam, he motioned in the direction of a highway turnout that overlooked the wildlife refuge. Hannah looked back up at him with a doting smile as she recognized the spot where Adam had proposed to her two years before.

Emily sat on a rock next to Kelsey. Kelsey nudged her and motioned toward Josh and Adam before asking, "Have those two always been so competitive?"

Emily and Hannah brayed and rolled their eyes in unison. "It will never end," Emily said. "Someday, when they're ninety years old and both in a retirement home, they'll still be battling over some inane game of dominoes or backgammon or some such nonsense."

Justin could suddenly be heard panting as he eased up to the stopping point. He slowly moseyed up to the overlook, took a gander at the view, and nodded to himself. Sweat was still rolling off his brow and onto his thick rimmed glasses. He plopped down on a log and sat still, with his wrists resting on his knees and his head lowered. "Sorry," he mumbled.

Emily waved her hand and whispered, "You're fine."

Kelsey got up, walked over, and sat next to Justin, to his right. She put her left arm around him. His eyes were suddenly held by hers as she sang the same song she had been crooning on the steep ascent. She squeezed him playfully. Justin was way too exhausted to feel uncomfortable. "Teach me something," she said enthusiastically.

"Kelsey, I don't know anything."

Kelsey looked over at Adam and asked, "What was I supposed to ask him?"

"Uranium enrichment," Adam replied, without hesitation.

"Alright," Kelsey said, snuggling up closer to Justin. She reached her hand farther around his shoulders. "Justin," she said, firmly and with feigned enthusiasm, "what's uranium enrichment?"

Justin smiled. He stared over at Adam and said, "Really?" Emily, Hannah, and Josh sat silently, anxious to eavesdrop on the discussion and Justin's exchange with Kelsey.

Justin rolled his eyes and having finally gotten his breath back, he adjusted himself on the log and sat up. Kelsey pulled away a bit and shifted slightly to look right into his eyes. "Okay," Justin started, "for a nuclear reaction to occur as needed for a nuclear weapon, nuclear power generation, or say, a nuclear submarine, a rare isotope of Uranium is needed."

"Isotope?"

"A different form of the element that has a different number of neutrons."

Kelsey rolled eyes and mumbled, "Okay, okay."

"Uranium that is mined consists primarily of Uranium-238 – over ninety-nine percent. Uranium has an atomic number of 92, meaning ninety-two protons."

"Okay, ninety-two protons," Kelsey said playfully.

"But, most of that Uranium that is found, that Uranium-238, has 146 neutrons while less than one percent of the mined uranium, which is more reactive, Uranium-235, has 143 neutrons."

"Adam, what the hell?" Kelsey barked. Adam smiled back at her. He then raised his eyebrows and tilted his head as he stared back. Everyone else was deadpan. Kelsey sighed deeply. "Okay, why is Uranium-235 more reactive?"

"Uranium-235 is known as a fissile isotope, in that after an initial reaction is triggered with a free neutron, a Uranium-235 atom will split into two separate atoms and emit neutrons at high speeds, along with a large amount of energy. If the uranium is enriched, being that there is a high percentage of the fissile Uranium-235, the neutrons emitted when an atom splits will incite new fission reactions with other Uranium-235 atoms, releasing more and more energy." Justin turned his head and looked right at Kelsey. "Boom," he said whimsically while raising his eyebrows, "lo, you got a nuclear chain reaction."

"You split the atom?"

"Yep," Justin replied, pursing his lips. "You've seen the videos of the mushroom clouds."

"Yeah, yeah," Kelsey said, looking over at Hannah. "They tested this down in New Mexico." Hannah and Emily winked at each other.

"Okay, so, there's a whole process used to produce the enriched uranium that has the high level of Uranium-235 needed for a nuclear weapon."

Kelsey slouched and her eyelids sank causing Justin to pause. He looked at her as if he was waiting for a comment. "Go on," she said as she slowly leaned over and rested her head against his shoulder causing his breath to hitch. His eyes widened. Adam, Josh, Hannah, and Emily made an effort to not look and sat quietly digging their boots in the dirt. After a few seconds of awkward silence, Cody lay beside Josh and closed his eyes. Eventually, Adam finally looked at Justin and held out his hand, palm up.

"Mined uranium ore," Justin continued with an edgy deflection in his voice. "By the way, you know a significant amount of uranium ore was mined in western Colorado." Justin pulled his arm back and put it around Kelsey's shoulder. "Anyway, the uranium ore is crushed and processed with solutions to leech out the uranium. The final product, referred to as yellow cake, consists, again, mostly of Uranium-238, which is not as radioactive."

"I like yellow cake," Kelsey said softly, "with chocolate icing." Hannah and Emily, both looking down at their boots, cracked smiles over the bit of levity Kelsey added to the discussion.

"Fluorine is added to the yellow cake that creates a gas, uranium hexafluoride, which can be enriched to yield a product with higher levels of Uranium-235, typically using centrifuges." Justin pivoted his head slightly toward Kelsey. "Remember using centrifuges in chemistry lab?"

"No," Kelsey said as she pulled her head up. Kelsey grimaced as she turned towards Adam and screamed, "Adam, what the hell? Why did you want me to ask about this?"

Josh and Hannah laughed as Adam grinned. They couldn't hold their deadpan expressions any longer.

"Centrifuges," Justin went on as he pulled his arm off Kelsey's shoulder, "involve rotating cylinders where the heavier gas molecules containing the U-238 isotopes get separated, toward the outer portion of the cylinders, from the molecules containing U-235 isotopes."

"Adam!" Kelsey yelled again with a scraping voice as she stood up and dusted off the seat of her pants.

"Kelsey," Justin said, "Adam wants us to talk to about the politics of enriching Uranium."

"No, not now," Josh said. "Come on, let's motor up a bit farther."

Josh hiked on up the trail as Kelsey shook her head and stared at Adam.

"Okay, okay," Adam said, chuckling. "I'll explain why later. I will. I promise." Adam darted off after Josh.

Hannah stepped over and gave Kelsey a hug and then pulled her toward the trail. Emily and Justin filed in behind them.

They all proceeded quietly up the trail and became separated as the narrower path with several switchbacks traversed a shaded, steep slope densely vegetated with old growth spruce trees and mature lodgepole pines. They passed three other groups heading down, each group politely stepping aside for uphill hikers. Most other hikers on the mountain had gotten an earlier start, but the weather was still fair and there was no apparent threat for a storm.

After twenty minutes of grinding their way up the slope, Hannah called up to Kelsey. Kelsey stopped and turned around. Hannah was breathing heavily as she said, "Justin's having a little trouble keeping up. Would you please hang back and talk to him?" Kelsey groaned. "Kelsey, I swear I'm not trying to force him on you. I think he may have felt a little dejected after you dismissed his little talk back there."

Kelsey sighed deeply and stepped gingerly off to the side of the path to let Hannah proceed, and as Emily passed, Kelsey smacked Emily firmly on the bottom and said, "You got a nice tush, girlfriend." Emily was too enervated to respond. Kelsey sat, on a large root protruding through the slope by the edge of the trail, and drank from the steel water bottle she had been carrying in her hand since the last stop.

A couple minutes passed. Justin was panting heavily as he walked up. He noticed Kelsey was mumbling indistinctly to herself and repeatedly clenching her teeth on the side of her hand. He stopped, his breathing intense and uncontrollable as the air whistled through his teeth. He squinted and gazed up at the full canopy of tree limbs blocking the sun. Kelsey continued with her inaudible utterings before Justin finally blurted out, "What are you doing?"

Startled, she almost dropped her water bottle. After a couple seconds, she regained awareness and slowly stood up. Justin was breathing steadily as she stepped up to him and used her fingers to fix his hair that was dripping with sweat. His brow was furrowed as he looked into her eyes. She put her arm around him. "I didn't mean to dismiss your little lecture back there," she said. "It was good." Justin leaned down and put his hands on his knees, and even though his shirt was soaked with sweat, Kelsey rubbed her hand on his back.

"You can go on," he said. "I'll get there."

"We're fine. It's not a race. It's a beautiful day. We got nowhere to be."

They stood quietly for a minute as Justin slowly got his breath back. Kelsey sat down again in the same spot. "Sit," she commanded, motioning to her right. Justin slowly sat and pulled out a new bottle of sports drink from his pack. He drank half the bottle in four gulps.

"Kelsey," Justin said as his breathing returned to normal, "I talk to myself sometimes."

Kelsey turned away. "Alright, what should I do?" she asked, looking down the trail.

"What do you mean?" he asked, turning to look at her.

Kelsey shook her head. "Where should I go? Where should I be?" She looked down at her boots. "I don't feel like there's any place for me," she mumbled.

Justin looked at Kelsey inquisitively. He leaned down in an attempt to look into her eyes. "What are you talking about?"

"Justin, I don't enjoy doing the things I used to cherish. I no longer enjoy going to the places I used to love."

Justin tilted his head. "How could that be?"

"Ah," Kelsey groaned, kicking at the dirt on the trail. "I can confide in you, can't I? Can I tell you anything?"

Justin chuckled. "Kelsey, I know you're well aware that I'm capable of being exceedingly quiet." Kelsey smiled and her torso bobbed with mirth as he continued, "No, seriously, I'm not exactly the gossipy type and if you tell me to not tell anyone, you know I won't tell anyone, ever." He awkwardly put his hand on her shoulder. "I was really worried about you last winter. I'm still worried about you, but I don't even know why. I don't know what happened."

"I caught him."

"Who?"

"Brandon! My ex."

"Where? When?"

"With Britt!" she screamed. Justin shook his head slowly. "I knew he was there. I went over there and walked right into her place without knocking. I heard them and I barged in on them–"

"You can spare me the lurid details." Justin said, cocking his head. "He was dating her before you, right?"

"So!"

"I'm sorry. I'm sorry. I'm just surprised Britt would do that." Justin put his arm around her and she leaned into him slightly. "Kelsey, I'm sorry. It just irks me to know you would go for a guy like that." Justin sighed as he looked up at the thick trunk on an old spruce tree to his right. A gust of wind picked up and the whistle of the air blowing through the pines was loud, and the creaks were even louder from a leaning, dead pine tree that was rubbing against another tree. "Why would Britt go for a guy like that?" he mumbled to himself. Kelsey shoved him, stood up, and marched up the trail. Justin hopped up and hobbled after her, his legs clearly aching from the hike. His backpack was open and hanging loosely on one shoulder as he ran up behind her. He put both his arms around her and pulled on her tightly. "I'm sorry," he said softly. "Kelsey, I'm so sorry. Look, I don't even know what that feels like. It's never happened to me, and it hasn't been something I've ever had to deal with."

Kelsey was in shock as he squeezed her with both arms, under her breasts. Her eyes were wide open as she stood, dazed and riveted, not breathing, and her head turned to the side, but she couldn't see him. As she eventually took a breath, she felt him press up against her. He rested his head against her shoulder blade and continued to pull on her. After several seconds, she slowly grabbed his right arm and gently pulled it away as she started to turn around.

"Come on, let's go," he blurted out as he released his grasp and nudged past her.

Kelsey was in a trance. For several seconds, she watched him lumber up the hill, slightly favoring his right leg. She stood still and watched until he disappeared from view over the next rise and behind two large spruce trees. She was able to catch up to him within seconds, and after they both settled into Justin's hiking rate, Justin, gasping for air, asked, "So you never told anyone?"

"No."

"Why?"

"I don't know."

"I'm going to frickin' kill him."

"Justin, you promised!"

"Okay," he grumbled, "as if I could do anything anyway."

Kelsey chortled. "I don't know. Some people are kind of scared of you, Justin. Seriously, some people think you might be crazy and don't know what you might do." Justin was still breathing heavily but was expressionless. "Do you remember my old boyfriend, Luke?" Kelsey asked. "I moved here from Texas with him."

"No."

"He cheated on me too. He moved up to Wyoming with her."

"Okay, Kelsey, I am sorry, but something else is going on. I'm not sure you have any qualms about being free from Brandon. I know that doesn't make you feel any better about the incident, but you're a beautiful, strong, empowered woman and should be able to get past this. Also, if I have the timeline right, you and Luke were done a long time ago. You're simply picking the wrong people." Justin sighed and continued, "We both know Adam and Hannah want us to talk, but I need to know what else is going on. I gave you my word and I promise you I will never tell anyone anything, but please talk to me."

Kelsey reached up and grabbed his arm. "Have you ever been depressed?"

"Sure," he said, standing sideways on the trail.

"I don't think you know what I'm talking about. I'm not talking about grief. I'm talking about despair."

Justin turned sideways to directly face her. Standing higher up on the trail, her head was about a foot lower than his. He ogled her light brown eyes. "Hey, I've been there," he said softly.

Kelsey stepped up the narrow path and was standing next to him, her face even with his and their eyes inches apart. "You explain it to me then."

"Alright, let me think about it, but I also need you to talk to me."

As she looked into his brown eyes, she reached up with both hands and wiped several drips of sweat off his eyebrows and slid her hands down over his cheeks.

"Alright, let's go," she mumbled.

Justin was moving slowly again with his breathing labored. Kelsey stayed with him and not having any difficulty with the pace, she began singing to herself again. After about fifteen minutes of moving up the steeper ascent, they reached tree line and squeaks from pika could be heard. Justin looked around persistently but was unable to spot any of the little mammals.

After a few more minutes of trudging through two thick fields of alpine wildflowers, they spotted Adam, Hannah, Josh, and Emily, all seated at the beginning of a rock field, waiting such that they would all be together as they navigated the talus slope. Adam was sitting on a large rock behind Josh, who was sitting low on some bedrock, and Adam was harassing Josh over his cheap hiking boots. Hannah was seated on a log with Cody by her feet, and Emily sat next to her, holding Josh's camera as she listened intently to Hannah comment on the different types of wildflowers in the field below.

Justin plopped down near Adam. Nobody made eye contact with him as he slowly crossed his legs and grimaced, pulling his backpack off his shoulders to grab his sport drink. Kelsey sat close to Hannah and rubbed up against her. As Hannah continued conversing with Emily, she reached over and put her hand on Kelsey's knee and Kelsey slowly leaned her head against Hannah's shoulder. Hannah and Emily continued whispering to each other, commenting over the beauty of the bellflowers, lupines, asters, geraniums, and penstemons.

Emily held up Josh's camera and took several photographs, and as she zoomed in close to an individual bunch of flowers, Hannah whispered, "Do you see any wallflowers?"

"There's your wallflower right there," Adam blurted out, pointing at Justin.

Hannah and Emily didn't turn their heads. "How about any wood nymphs?" Hannah asked softly.

"There's your wood nymph," Josh said, pointing at Kelsey.

Kelsey lifted her head off Hannah's shoulder, curled her lip in disdain, and spluttered, "I'm not a wood nymph."

Emily stared over at Josh and whispered, "Apologize."

"Sorry," Josh said before looking at Adam with a shrug.

"I would say she's closer to a Yreka Phlox," Justin suddenly said, having gotten his breath back. Emily and Hannah simultaneously looked over at him. "It's an endangered wildflower you're not going to see here. They're very beautiful but very rare."

"Alright, alright," Kelsey blurted out with a hoarse voice, "you're about to make me barf." Kelsey looked at Adam and said, "Adam, tell me about the politics of Uranium isotopes." Emily groaned and rolled her eyes as she swung her head away and started snapping photos again. Hannah stared down at her palm and started pinching to try to remove a large splinter she picked up at some point along the way.

"Well," Adam said, "okay, here's the problem. The use of nuclear weapons is not an option." Josh became still as he listened intently. Adam repeated, "The use of nuclear weapons is simply not an option. The scientists that figured it all out and created that first mushroom cloud down in New Mexico–"

"At the Trinity Site," Kelsey interjected.

"Yeah. They knew. They were immediately telling themselves, 'What have we done?'" Josh looked down and whacked a stick against his boot. "We know," Adam went on. "The U.S. knows. Russia knows. Everyone knows. Using a nuclear weapon is not an option. But the technology and knowledge to develop the weapons has become more commonly known, and rogue regimes, that historically exhibited behavior destructive to the basic well-being of the world's population, cannot come into possession of a nuclear weapon."

"What they really need to understand," Josh chimed in, "is that it wouldn't accomplish anything for them."

Emily sighed and reached over for Hannah's hand, "I'll get it," she whispered as she put her face down close to Hannah's hand and started pinching at the splinter.

"We understand," Josh went on, "that these rogue states are looking for respect from the rest of the world, but developing a nuclear weapon is a hostile act. Having a nuclear weapon will not accomplish anything for them and using a nuclear weapon is certainly not an option. They could build up their own national defense and receive so much more respect if, at the same time, they outwardly acknowledged, to themselves, to their citizens, and to the rest of the world, that the use of nuclear weapons is not an option."

"We have them," Kelsey said.

"Yes," Josh said. "Yes, and that's another topic. Efforts need to continue to reduce the stockpile of nuclear weapons and blend down the supply of highly enriched uranium, the weapons grade uranium Justin talked about."

"Also," Adam said, "we need to track all the yellow cake in the world."

Hannah perked up, and with a wry smile, she said, "I also like yellow cake with chocolate icing." Kelsey looked over at Hannah and smiled playfully.

"It should all be handled diplomatically, if possible," Josh said.

"If possible," Adam concurred, "but the U.S. is also working with other nations to assure rogue states do not acquire or develop the technology to create a nuclear weapon, and it must be known that the use of force is an option."

"How?" Kelsey asked.

"Blow up their centrifuges."

Josh shook his head. "Really?" he asked, turning to look at Adam.

"I hope not," Adam replied, "but–"

"Ah, you've been spending too much time with Drew."

Emily suddenly called, "Got it," and she flicked the large splinter from her fingernails. With a sigh of relief, she groaned, "Argh."

"Kelsey," Josh started, "the paramount thing to understand, is that it doesn't do the rogue states any good to have a nuclear weapon. They can't use it. If they were to use it, absolutely nothing good would come from it for their regime, their citizens, or anyone in the world."

"They could threaten to use it," Kelsey said.

"But we've been through that. There's no need for any nation to be involved in a Cold War again."

"Alright, alright," Emily said as she stood up, "I'm going to head up." Josh and Adam were quick to put on their backpacks and managed to dash ahead of Emily. Kelsey dusted off her pants and slowly stepped in line behind them.

Justin was moving slowly to get his backpack on, and Hannah politely took her time to wait. As soon as the others were several steps up the trail, Justin stepped toward Hannah and whispered, "Can I ask you a question?"

"Yeah, what's up?"

"You have to tell me. What happened with Kelsey, that night, back in January?"

Hannah quickly spun her head around to look up toward Kelsey. After she paused for a few seconds, she said, "She had a rough night. I really don't know what happened, something with Brandon. Anyway, she was walking down the middle of the highway, wearing nothing but a t-shirt, at 2:00 a.m."

"In January?"

"Yeah."

"at 2:00 a.m.?"

"Yes, Justin, it was probably 15 below. Thankfully, her neighbor, Kyle, happened to be driving by and saw her. He picked her up and took her to the emergency room."

"Hannah, I know we don't need to discuss the science of hypothermia, but if she had been out there very long, she seriously could have frozen to death?"

"I believe that was the intent. She was pretty messed up. Thankfully, I don't think she was out there more than twenty minutes or so, but we don't know for sure. I can't remember exactly how low her body temperature got, but she had legitimate hypothermia and ended up with some frostbite blisters on her toes. She still has a scar on one of her toes. Justin, I don't mind divulging this to you because I know you won't talk about it."

"No, no," Justin said, knitting his brow as he looked up at Kelsey on the trail. "Is it still a concern?"

"I don't know. Come on, let's go."

As they stepped up the trail, Justin said, "You can go ahead. I'm right behind you. There's no way I can keep up with all of you. Seriously, just go. We're above tree line now, so you'll all be able to see me the entire time." Hannah patted his shoulder and walked on.

They all made their way through the rock field and were less winded by the effort as they moved slowly and gingerly, stepping on large rocks and focusing on each step to assure they stayed on the trail that was marked by cairns, large piles of rocks strategically maintained at each turn. They passed seven other groups of hikers coming down the talus slope.

As Justin reached the top of the rock field, Kelsey was waiting. "Hey, wizard, I got a question for you, what's with the rock field?"

Justin stopped and took several seconds to get his breath back as he turned and scanned the talus. "Remnants from the end of the last ice age," he finally said. "With the repeated freezing and thawing of water in the mountain rock, large rocks broke off and slid, ultimately settling right there above tree line."

"It's not going to move on us, is it?"

"Nah."

Kelsey nodded as she patted him lightly on the arm. They progressed over the alpine tundra and up the last section of the trail to the peak of Mount Preston. The final trek was not steep, but at over thirteen thousand feet above sea level, the air was much thinner and Kelsey was quickly ahead of Justin again. Adam and Josh, raced to the top. Josh managed to stay in front, but Adam was on his heels till the end.

One other group was already seated on the rocky peak that included Kyle, exhibiting his typical stolid demeanor. Adam and Josh sat on separate rocks. A stiff breeze was blowing, and Emily immediately snuggled up to Josh as soon as she arrived. They both began eating two bananas Josh pulled from his backpack. As Hannah sat by Adam, he tossed one of the Knoxville subs in the air. She barely caught the sandwich that was wrapped tightly in foil. Adam threw another sandwich toward Josh and Emily. Hannah called Cody over to her, and after some persistent commands, she managed to get him to sit, the rocks making for an awkward resting place. Kelsey strolled up behind them and continued several feet farther to sit by herself.

They all sat facing south in what was probably the best possible spot to take in the splendor of the entire Spruce Creek valley. The river could be seen starting with the headwaters to the left. Both the north fork and south fork of the creek could be followed down to their confluence, and the meanders of the main stream could be viewed continuing through its thick, healthy riparian corridor as it snaked its way west down the valley and flowed north toward Lake Labash. Back to the left, all the front-side runs at the ski resort were visible, and they could see the entire Wallace Gulch valley to the south. The summit of Higgins Peak was below them but towering up to the east where the tundra above tree line was particularly green that summer due to copious amount of June rain received from the good monsoon season moisture that came up from the Gulf of Mexico and the Pacific Ocean.

Justin joined them several minutes later. As he stepped by Adam, Adam handed him two Knoxville subs. Justin stepped further along the peak toward Kelsey. He paused as he stood by her. She was humming to herself as he motioned his hand, inquiring if he could sit by her. There was barely enough room on the rock for both of them, but Kelsey didn't resist. As he sat, he slowly pulled off his backpack and pulled out his sport drink. He handed one of the subs to Kelsey. She ripped open the foil and began devouring the prize with large bites. She gazed back into Justin's eyes while she chewed. Without asking, she reached over and grabbed his sports drink and took a big gulp.

Justin suddenly looked forward and gasped. A female mountain goat with two kids walked into view from the slope below. The goats were about forty feet away, but Justin was still uneasy. Kelsey furrowed her brow as she watched him. "Are you scared of goats?" she asked with her mouth full. Justin shrugged but was fidgeting and poised to get up.

Hannah put her arm around Cody's neck and softly shushed as she maintained a firm hold on his collar. Cody watched the goats intently and whimpered but didn't budge. Kelsey picked up a rock and tossed it gently, the rock landing halfway between them and the nanny goat. The nanny goat, with her beard and short black horns, turned to walk in front of Josh, Emily, and the others. The kids scurried along behind her. The nanny goat's coat was scruffy with about a quarter of her winter wool still not shed.

Everyone sat silently as they watched the goats march in front of them. The goats then moved steadily across the hiking trail and proceeded to the backside of the mountain. Despite the precipitous drop-off, the goats walked down the steep slope without hesitation and disappeared out of view. Justin noticed Kelsey's neighbor, Kyle. Justin froze, his mouth full from a bite of his hoagie. He stared right at Kyle for several seconds before he continued chewing again. He slowly turned his head back and looked at Kelsey. After looking back at Kyle, he looked at Kelsey again. Justin slouched slightly as he swallowed the bite of his sandwich and squinted at Kelsey.

"What?" she asked.

Justin didn't respond.

Chapter 5 – Room for Science at the Java Alley

The morning sun shined bright through the front windows at the Java Alley, the local coffee shop in the main village of the Spruce Creek Resort. Hannah, with her back to the front door, sat on an old couch in the darker, sunken section at the rear of the shop and leaned over a coffee table as she thumbed through the daily edition of the local Spruce Creek News. Cody lay outside but with his back abutting the front door which was propped open by a stone. He barely left enough room for people to step around him as they entered the shop, but most of the regular patrons knew Cody and were plenty happy to see him. While Cody couldn't see Hannah, his eyes were locked on Emily as she stood at the front of the shop, browsing the latest assortment of books for sale and displayed along the right side wall, opposite the main counter.

The store was somewhat hectic as seven customers waited in line to place take-out orders for drinks and pastries, and four employees worked frantically while six other patrons waited to receive their orders. All the customers were taking their food and drinks outside that warmer Monday morning to sit at the tables in front of the shop or elsewhere in the plaza, but with the doors and windows completely open, it also felt like an al fresco environment inside.

"Emily," Hannah suddenly called. Cody immediately raised his head, the tags on his collar jingling. "We're in the paper," Hannah commented loudly. Emily nodded nonchalantly as she continued to read the back of a book she had grabbed off the shelf.

Pulling the paper up close to her face, Hannah softly mumbled, "I don't remember seeing Josh take this picture." It was a photograph of all of them as they began their descent from Mount Preston the day before. The photo afforded an awe-inspiring, panoramic view of the mountains to the west of Mount Preston.

The lead server at the shop walked swiftly out from behind the counter with Hannah's and Emily's drinks as an older retired couple politely stepped out of her way. The server, as amiable as they come, stepped around a large coffee roaster to the left and continued down three steps to the sunken seating section in the back. Hannah was the only person in the area. Bluegrass music, emanating from small speakers in the corners of the seating area, could be heard faintly over the chatter from the customers in the front of the shop. Hannah didn't look up as the server placed Emily's caffe latte and Hannah's glass of brewed decaffeinated tea on the table. "Thank you," Emily said sweetly as she scuttled down the steps. The server returned her signature cherubic smile as Emily passed.

"Do you still hate her?" Emily whispered as she sat down in an old, creaky, wooden chair.

"No, I don't hate her."

"Adam still comes in here, right?"

"Yes, it's fine."

"They were nothing but friends," Emily affirmed, "not even that."

"I know," Hannah said as she maintained focus on her newspaper.

The server was Britt, now twenty-four years old. She had befriended Adam shortly before Adam and Hannah had become engaged. Emily took a sip of her caffe latte and watched Britt, pausing by the counter to chat with the retired couple. Britt, five-feet six inches tall with long, black hair and beautiful, flawless skin was donning a ponytail that morning that was pulled over her right shoulder.

"You know, I hate Kelsey," Emily suddenly said.

Hannah sat up and gazed at Emily. "What? Why?"

Emily scoffed. "Josh was totally ogling her yesterday."

Hannah smiled and waved her hand. "So was Adam." Hannah kept chuckling. "I'm not too worried about it. It is funny how they think they're being so stealth about it when it's so obvious."

Emily shook her head. "I'm more disgusted with Kelsey. She's so bright and beautiful, just like that Phlox wildflower or whatever it was Justin called it. But she's being such an idiot."

"I know." Hannah said, folding up the newspaper and pushing it toward the center of the table.

"How could she ever be sad? She's so pretty and so strong. She could do anything if she changed her perspective."

Hannah picked up her decaffeinated tea with two hands, took a gentle sip, and leaned back on the sofa. "You know, she has no girlfriends. Actually, all girls hate her."

"Well, for one, they can't stand how guys have such a propensity to lose themselves over her."

Hannah laughed and added, "And she doesn't even have to do anything! She's not coquettish at all, and she doesn't exactly pour on the charm. There isn't a whole lot of grace being exhibited there. Her boss, Drew, says that when she's working on a site, she'll be all sweaty and dirty and slovenly, and the other fellas on the crew will still be checking her out all day long."

"Maybe that's why I hate her," Emily said. "I don't know." Emily raised her head and eyeballed some kids who had sat next to Cody. As they petted him, they made it even more difficult for customers to step into the shop. "No," Emily went on, "it's how Kelsey carries herself. I would like her if she was a little more old fashioned. She sells out. She's so free-spirited with her wanton, licentious lifestyle and it makes me sick how guys go limp when they're around girls like that. Half the guys at the North Fork show up just hoping she'll be there and so they can get another look at her."

Emily suddenly gulped. She reached over, tapped Hannah on the arm, and motioned her head toward the front door. Justin had walked in by himself, holding a scientific journal, and in signature fashion, he shifted his feet quickly and gauchely as he walked toward the back of the shop. As he started down the steps, he noticed Hannah and Emily and froze. His eyes danced around anxiously.

"Really?" Hannah said. "After all that time we spent together yesterday, you're still nervous?" Justin shrugged and strode over to a small table on the other side of the sunken seating area, as far away from Hannah and Emily as possible. When he peered over at them, Hannah chuckled and said, "You are an enigma, Justin." Emily, with her back to him, give an emotionless nod and turned back toward Hannah. Justin, now with his back to the front door, sat in a flimsy, wooden chair and exhaled as he became ensconced in the aroma of fresh pastries and roasted coffee beans.

"Did you have a good time yesterday?" Hannah asked.

"Yeah," he replied, his voice cracking, "I guess I need to work on my conditioning, but yes, it was a lot of fun. Thanks for inviting me."

"What are you researching these days?"

"Bumble bees," he replied. Emily furrowed her brow as she turned to look at him.

"What's going on with the bumble bees?" Hannah asked.

"Their tongues are shrinking." Emily chuckled as she looked back at Hannah. Justin laughed along as he continued, "I'm serious. Okay, so, fewer flowers are now available at higher elevations throughout the Rocky Mountains, theoretically due to climate change, and the bumble bee population is having to adapt to the resulting changes to the available sources for nectar. It really is interesting, the data show that the length of their tongues is now different. The indication is that their tongues have changed to what's needed for the available flowers." Hannah's and Emily's eyes were wide open as they turned and stared at each other. Their foreheads crinkled as they tried to hold back their smiles.

Britt walked down the steps. She had a blueberry muffin on a small saucer and a cup of coffee in a ceramic Java Alley mug. She had already added the perfect amount of sugar and creamer for Justin's coffee. "Justin," Britt blurted out, "you're talking!" Hannah and Emily responded with gales of laughter which provoked a dirty look from Justin. Britt set the muffin and coffee on his table. "Wow, you have nice voice, Justin. It's like one of those deep, radio voices."

"Thanks," Justin whispered. As Britt turned to walk away, she lightly patted her hand on the side of his head and ran two fingers through his shaggy hair. She flashed an affable smile at Emily.

"Anyway," Justin continued, "with a reduction in the supply of mountain flowers, the bumble bee population is adapting to the change. We're analyzing the data further."

"Huh," Hannah grunted, keenly.

The two tags on Cody's collar could suddenly be heard jingling at the top of the steps. Hannah whipped her head around. "Hey," she said, "what are you doing? Go back outside." Hannah gave Cody a stern look and firmly repeated, "Go back outside and lie down." Cody whimpered. "Go on," Hannah commanded. Cody slowly turned around and lumbered back toward the door as all the other customers watched. Cody lay down in the same spot against the door but facing away from the shop.

"Justin," Emily said, somewhat coldly, "now that you've spent some time with Kelsey, what would you say is going on with her?"

"Gosh," Justin started as he slouched in his chair. "I don't know." He stared down at the floor for a few seconds before looking up at Emily. "I can tell you this: she can't stand being alone. She can't stand it for one minute." He hemmed and hawed. "Everything she's doing in this rut she's in, tying on a buzz every night, getting together with boys, stumbling around in the wee hours of the morning. She's looking from some sort of escape from reality or from the memories of her past or maybe from her normal self. It's her personality. She can't take being alone." Justin sat up in his chair. "When did her roommate start staying over at her boyfriend's place full time, leaving Kelsey at home by herself every night?"

"I don't know," Hannah replied. "Let's see, I guess Sadie's been serious with her boyfriend for about a year now."

"Sadie wasn't there that night back in January when–"

"No," Hannah interjected.

Justin smiled as he asked, "Do you remember those particular kids in high school that couldn't walk down the hall by themselves? They were popular, but they would rather walk down the hall with a nerd than walk by themselves. They would grab anyone and tell them to tag along on the route to their next class so they wouldn't have to walk alone." Hannah and Emily smiled at each other. "Does the timing match?" Justin asked. "Did things get bad for Kelsey around the same time that Sadie left and Kelsey was coming home to an empty apartment every night?"

"Not necessarily," Hannah replied.

"Well, have you ever seen Kelsey out alone? Out shopping for groceries by herself? Picking up her mail at the post office by herself? Anywhere?"

"Guess not."

"So, on the hike yesterday, when she was waiting for me by herself, she was biting her hand and talking to herself. I assume she had only been there for a couple minutes, but she had already fallen into a bad place. Ranting and raving under her breath."

"Yeah, I've seen it," Hannah said.

Emily exhaled and slowly muttered, "Crazy Kelsey."

"Maybe it's not as simple as having a personality where she can't handle being alone," Justin started but clammed up as he noticed Britt walking down the steps. She started grabbing empty cups and saucers off other tables. She was smiling again after she heard Justin talking. "But she wants to get away from herself," Justin continued, anxiously. "I don't know why. Maybe she regrets the way she's lived her life. Maybe she has nothing but vivid memories of her past, those moments after she's made some horrible decisions. I'm assuming that as soon as she ties on a buzz and gets together with a boy, the bad memories of her tempestuous past fade, the pangs of remorse subside, and she's in a new exhilarating moment." Britt's face became expressionless as she listened to Justin's comments. He took a bite of his muffin. "I hear she's a good worker," he added with his mouth full. "When she's working, doing manual labor, and lost in a task, the memories aren't there."

"I don't know," Hannah said. "I think it's more complicated than that. I'm not arguing that it's a factor, but that deal with Brandon was a major issue." Britt abruptly lurched forward, and the empty dishes in her hands clanged as they fell against her belly. Emily, bemused, watched Britt closely as she scampered up the steps with the dishes rattling against her tummy. She knocked into a couple patrons before darting behind the counter.

Hannah leaned over and whispered, "She used to go out with Brandon before he dated Kelsey."

"Yeah, yeah, I know," Emily said, still furrowing her brow as she scrutinized Britt.

Emily watched Britt intently as Justin and Hannah took sips of their beverages. Emily reached over, tapped Hannah, and motioned her head toward the front door. Kelsey's roommate, Sadie Halper, had walked in, and as soon as Sadie saw Hannah, she scuttled down the steps. "Thanks for cleaning my home," Sadie said with a laugh.

"It wasn't me," Hannah replied. "It was Adam." Sadie stepped around Emily, rubbing her hand along her shoulder, and sat in an adjacent chair. Hannah leaned forward and whispered, "Sometimes I can be passive aggressive, play off Adam's obsessive compulsive tendencies, and get him to clean without hardly saying anything."

"Hannah," Emily yelled.

"I know," Hannah responded. "I don't do it often," Hannah whispered, "but I can leave the kitchen dirty and promise I'll clean it up before I go to bed, and he'll go ahead take care of it because he just can't take it."

Sadie, originally from New York, worked for the resort helping to organize special events such as weddings, festivals, and concerts. She was wearing little makeup that morning, and at twenty-eight years old, little makeup was needed with her youthful, light brown complexion. She was dressed for the start of her work day in tan slacks and a black, long-sleeved, button-down, collared shirt with the Spruce Creek Resort logo on the left breast.

"I heard you had a good hike," Sadie said.

"Yeah, it was nice," Hannah replied. Sadie smiled as she looked over at Justin who had buried his head in his professional journal. She whipped her head back toward Hannah and motioned her thumb in his direction. "Yes," Hannah responded, "Justin went with us." Justin didn't look up. "We had a really nice time."

"Justin," Sadie said, "I heard you and Kelsey had a good talk yesterday." Justin peered up at her. Sadie looked back at him with a ravishing, exotic gaze that was natural for her. With the dimmer light in the back of the shop, her dark brown eyes appeared black. Justin shrugged nervously. "I went home to do some laundry last night, and Justin, Kelsey was doting on you the entire time!" Justin dropped his head low and refocused on his journal. Sadie turned back toward Hannah, shook her head, and motioned her thumb toward him again.

"He's fine," Hannah said. "Everything's great."

Britt walked down the steps and handed Sadie a drink in a to-go cup. Sadie promptly gave her a couple dollars. Sadie's frizzy, crinkled, black hair bounced as she waved at Britt and whispered, "Keep it."

"Hey," Sadie said before taking a quick sip of her drink, "let me know if there's anything I can do to help, with Kelsey. You know I tried. I gave her some serious, healthy doses of tough love last spring. You know I tell her I love her every time I see her, but we're on such different wavelengths, I wonder if I only make it worse."

"Okay, I will. We're going to beat this, whatever it is."

"Well, I got to get," Sadie said, standing up. She ran her hand over Emily's shoulder as she stepped by and then leaned down to hug Hannah lightly. "See you later," she whispered. "Tell Adam I said thanks for cleaning." As Sadie started up the steps, she glanced over at Justin and coquettishly said, "Bye Justin." He didn't look up but elevated his hand timidly. After she walked up the steps, Justin finally looked up and watched her as she proceeded toward the door and then took a long stride to step over Cody.

"She is beautiful," Hannah said. "I don't blame you for being nervous."

"Emily," Justin said, "what's our next topic of discussion for Kelsey? I need to know so I'll be prepared. I lucked out with the last two topics."

"I don't know. Don't ask me. I haven't been involved in this." Justin kept staring at her as he took a bite of his muffin and slowly chewed. "Okay, okay, hold on," Emily said, wiggling her head in thought, "how about evolution and the Big Bang." Justin perked up. His posture was suddenly perfect.

"Emily," Hannah yelled, "you don't subscribe to that pagan nonsense, do you?"

Justin's eyes popped. He turned and looked askance at Hannah. He slowly stood up, walked over, and sat on the sofa right next to her. His leg was pressing against her leg, and she shifted in discomfort. "You don't believe in evolution?" he asked.

"Oh," Hannah groaned, "Emily, what have you done?"

"Hannah?" Justin droned.

"Justin, I don't need you to explain evolution or the Big Bang to me. I know the theories." Justin leaned back on the sofa and gazed at her. Hannah shifted farther away. "Justin, would you–"

"Here's the deal," he interjected. Hannah sighed and opened her eyes real big as she looked over at Emily. "Hannah, there has got to be more acceptance of science in the church. It doesn't need to construed as a some sort of paradigm shift and it certainly doesn't need to be summarily dismissed as a conflict to core beliefs. Science is not moving in to usurp the domain of religion."

"Thanks Emily," Hannah said, "I appreciate this."

Emily grimaced. "Apparently I hit a nerve."

"Justin," Hannah said, shifting again on the sofa, "seriously, would you–"

"Hannah, look, you can accept the immutable laws of science and still have faith in a divine creator. It simply requires you to have a little flexibility in your interpretation to make room for proven scientific concepts. There's no need to get bogged down over anything that might seem contradictory to your beliefs. It's merely a matter of not getting caught up in an entirely literal interpretation of the scripture. Hannah, I don't believe everything was meant to be taken so literally?"

"Emily," Hannah said, "you started this. Fix it, now!"

"Justin," Emily called.

"Hannah, of course, we know the value of the church in the community and the key role it plays in the lives of all families along with the value of faith to each individual, regardless of where they are with their faith. And we know that having a source for a moral code is so important to all societies and to everyone, regardless of their denomination, but to feel threatened at all by science and regular advancements in science is ridiculous. Science has proven to be so valuable to our daily lives, our quality of life, and our security."

"What about your bumble bees?" Hannah asked

"What about them?"

"Aerodynamically, they shouldn't be able to fly, right? But miraculously, they do."

"Hannah," Justin exclaimed, "that's a myth. Scientists fully understand how bumble bees are able to fly." Hannah groaned loudly as Justin went on, "Alright, let's talk about some details. What about the mountains all around us? We understand how plate tectonics caused the uplift which created our beautiful Colorado Rocky Mountains. It's a rudimentary concept. We also know that glaciers, that formed over ice ages, flowed down the mountains and carved out the jagged peaks. We know that volcanoes left old lava lakes that protected the flat tops from being eroded by rivers and glaciers. We can see it all, right in front of us, and we know how this all happened over millions of years! And it's visible, right in front of us, and people accept it until it's inconvenient, but then some abruptly dismiss it so they can continue to accept a literal interpretation of the Bible. They don't have to do that. Hannah, I'm not sure we were ever expected to accept a fully literal interpretation of everything in the Bible. Please know that it's possible for anyone to fully accept everything we know now as a result of scientific revolutions and still be at a good place with their deity."

"Deity?" Hannah muttered. "Emily!"

"Justin," Emily called loudly. Justin slowly rotated his head. "What's happening with all the butterflies?"

"The monarch butterflies?"

"Yeah."

"Well," Justin started as he shifted on the sofa to face Emily. Hannah seized the opportunity to shift farther away from Justin. "There are different theories. Deforestation in Mexico has impacted the availability of protective habitat where the butterflies spend their winters. Also, drought in their migratory zone has affected the availability of the nectar sources they need to survive. More importantly, I guess, is that the use of herbicides in the Midwest has decimated the amount of available milkweed, which is their primary food source and the place where the butterflies lay their eggs and caterpillars hatch out. The use of pesticides obviously hasn't helped either." Justin hemmed and hawed a bit. "I haven't actually studied it myself or analyzed the data."

"Justin," Hannah groaned, "would you please go back over to your table?" Justin scoffed, got up, and stormed over to his chair. He bridled his head as he sat down, grabbing his scientific journal and lifting his right leg up on his left knee. "I'm sorry," Hannah said softly.

"Actually," Emily said, "I need to go."

"Yeah, me too," Hannah added.

As they stood up, Justin kept his head down. Hannah stepped over to him and lowered her head in an attempt to get eye contact. "I'm sorry. Look, some people need their space, and you freak people out sometimes. I figured you would understand that as well as anyone."

"Fine."

"We're all going to the North Fork on Thursday. Maybe we'll see you there?" Justin shrugged. "I do appreciate your help with Kelsey. We're making progress. I'll think about everything you said, about Kelsey and science and bumble bees and whatnot. I promise."

As Emily walked up the steps, the front of the shop had cleared out. Britt was standing behind the counter checking her phone. "You'll look after our boy down there?" Emily asked.

"Sure, I'll take good care of him," Britt replied with a smile.

After Hannah and Emily departed, Britt walked down the steps toward Justin. Unprompted, he commenced talking, with his head down. "Britt, how can somebody that works in the oil industry believe that the universe is ten thousand years old?" Britt was expressionless as she slowly rotated her head back toward the front door. Cody was absolutely giddy, hopping back-and-forth in front of Hannah. "Scientists know," Justin went on, "that it takes much longer than that for crude oil to form from fossilized organic material into kerogen and then petroleum. People that work in the coal industry know that coal comes from plant material that accumulated in wetlands, decomposed, became buried, and compacted over millions of year. Yet some of these same people will subscribe to a literal interpretation of the scripture." Justin stared at the remainder of his muffin and slowly shook his head. Britt was wooden and moved quietly as she slowly turned and walked away without saying a word.

Chapter 6 – Executive Order for Hayes and Webb

Josh stood still, assessing the line for his drive at the sixth hole at the Spruce Creek disc golf course. Thunder rumbled faintly off to his left, though the sky was clear overhead. Adam and Drew turned to scan the darker clouds over the peaks to the west. The course, located three miles down the valley from the resort, on the north side of the highway and above an older complex of townhomes, consisted of a complete eighteen holes with lines to each basket passing through thickets of lodgepole pines, around isolated aspen groves, and over large, open areas with sagebrush. Elevations along the course varied by nearly four hundred feet which made for a challenging course to play, particularly on windy days, and also increased the amount of calories burned as players progressed from hole to hole. Higher locations on the course afforded dramatic views of the ski resort to the southeast, the majestic mountain range to the west, and Spruce Creek below as it meandered down the valley to Lake Labash.

A threesome in front of them just cleared the area around the sixth basket that was slightly uphill from the tee box. As the group disappeared into a thick collection of lodgepole pines, Josh, looking north, with Mount Preston towering in front of him, examined the line for his backhand throw one last time. He then took three quick steps and winged a soaring drive, well to the right of the line to the basket. Josh, Adam, and Drew, all wearing sunglasses, shorts, and t-shirts on that seventy degree late Wednesday afternoon, stood still, watching as Josh's disc flew farther to the right around a small group of pine trees. Josh winced as the disc began to tilt even more to the right but then finally eased back left, redirecting toward the sixth basket. As the disc lost momentum, the wind picked up and elevated the disc up another ten feet before it finally nosedived into some sagebrush.

"See it?" Adam asked.

"Yeah, I got it," Josh replied.

"So why do you always throw backhand while Adam throws forehand?" Drew asked.

"Ah, that's my comfort zone, I guess," Josh replied. "I don't know how Adam can throw those forehands so far."

"Heck," Adam said, "I can't throw a backhand more than a hundred feet." Adam looked at Josh and asked, "When you play tennis and a ball comes right at you, do you step to the right and hit a backhand or to the left and swing a forehand?"

"Backhand."

Adam thumbed to himself and said, "Forehand."

Adam stepped onto the concrete pad to tee off, and with little hesitation, he took three steps and slung a forehand drive well to left of the line to the basket. His disc stayed low but maintained its height, protected from the wind by the thick forest of pine trees to the left. The disc edged along the trees but managed to steer clear of any branches. After the disc passed through a narrow passage between two dead trees, it banked right, dropped hard, and landed about forty feet to the left of Josh's disc.

"Nice throw," Drew said. "Well, I guess I'm going to be buying beers tomorrow. Alright, I'm going to try a forehand this time."

As Drew stepped onto the concrete pad, the chains on the basket clinked behind them as a young couple, with an old, slow-moving chocolate Labrador, had thrown their last shots to close out the fifth hole. Drew took a couple more seconds and threw a forehand that zinged directly toward a stand of pine trees about sixty feet in front of the tee. His disc nailed the trunk of the first tree, head on, and with a resonating thud, the disc fell straight down.

They all quietly watched as the disc landed on its side and rolled wobbly over a bed of pine needles before coming to rest against a couple fallen branches. Drew sighed as they slowly picked up their disc bags, each containing a wide assortment of discs for driving, approach shots, and putting. Josh, being a consummate shutterbug, also had his camera bag in tow.

Drew walked directly up to his disc and after concluding he had no line through the pines for a level throw, he tomahawked his disc up through a high opening in the stand of trees. His disc made it through the high branches and floated farther, upside down, before landing about halfway between Adam's and Josh's discs.

They strolled on peacefully through the stand of pine trees and then through some spare sagebrush. They were in no hurry, for the pace of their game was ultimately dependent on the group ahead of them. "Yeah Adam," Drew said, resuming their discussion from earlier, "your boy, Hayes, is right. When Ms. Webb's working, she's great. Once she shows up, she busts her butt and she's totally focused on the task at hand." Drew smacked Adam on the shoulder. "It really is so noble what your wife is trying to do. There are several people that won't even talk to Ms. Webb anymore."

"I don't like that. I guess I understand why some people avoid her. I get it. As soon as she crosses that proverbial line, it's entirely her responsibility to get things sorted out. But in many regards, it's sad. The thing is, she's a human being!"

Drew shook his head and mumbled, "Ms. Webb and Mr. Hayes." Josh emitted a guttural laugh as Drew added, "The most extroverted chick I've ever known and the most introverted guy in the entire valley."

"I'm not sure he's that interested in her," Adam said. "I mean, sure, he's affected when she's around, like the rest of us, but there's no indication she's gotten to him. He doesn't fawn all over her the way others do."

"What's up with that?"

"I don't know. Actually, I could tell you an amusing story." Adam cleared his throat before he continued, "So I was riding my bike down the bike path about three weeks ago, and I came up on Justin, sitting on a rock by the creek, just off the path. He was holding a book, but man, was he in a zone, just staring into the stream. It appeared as if he was doing calculations in his head or something." Drew rolled his eyes as they all eased up to his disc. He grabbed it and threw it softly toward the basket with no intention of trying to make the shot but with sole intention of getting his disc to settle as close to the basket as possible and set up one last shot.

"Anyway," Adam continued as he walked over to his disc, "Justin assured me he was fine and laughed at himself. I guess he felt like he should explain, so he asked me if I thought he was a flake." Drew and Josh furrowed their brows as Adam paused to throw his disc. His disc skipped off the top of the basket but fell straight down, setting himself up for an easy final putt. "Anyway," Adam continued as they stepped over toward Josh's disc. "I guess one of the chicks that works at the research center with him completely lost it on him earlier that day. She went off on him in the cafeteria, in front of several other people, telling him he was the biggest flake in the entire Colorado high country."

"Well that's saying something," Drew said. "There are definitely some flakes up here. I sure know that from trying to find good employees."

"So I pried and was able to put together the story." Adam paused as Josh threw his disc which narrowly missed the basket but floated well past the basket. Josh cursed. "So," Adam continued, "Justin had apparently befriended this chick and would eat lunch with her a couple times a week. They e-mailed each other on occasion. He also met her for happy hour a couple times, but he didn't think anything of it. All they ever did was talk shop. They talked about the politics at the research center and funding, gossiped about all the administrative help, and shared findings from their research."

"Who is this girl?" Josh asked, speaking loudly as he walked past the basket toward his disc.

"I can't remember her name. I wouldn't guess you would know her. She lives over the pass in the next county. It sounds like she's cute, slim, but not so active, vegetarian, cerebral. I gather she lives one of those lives of austere isolation, which you would think would be right up Justin's alley. She plays violin in the orchestra in the summer and supposedly practices a lot."

"Anyway," Adam continued, "she obviously had become keen on him and thought there was much more to their lunch dates while Justin wasn't really thinking about her at all and saw her only as a work associate. After she flipped out on him, he was no doubt distressed and suddenly too nervous to talk to her, but he went to her office and tried to explain supposed flakes to her. He told her how some people battle serious insecurity, and in some cases, it gets to the point that they convince themselves that nobody would ever be interested in them. He also explained that some guys are flat out horrified of getting hurt. A guy might not want to fall for a girl only for her to flake out on him after he's become emotionally attached or, even worse, for her to cheat on him shortly after it gets serious. Also, apparently he didn't tell her this, but he talked to me about it. He noted that too many people look at a situation and figure that if it makes sense on paper, they should pursue it, but he doesn't believe in that. He only believes in pursuing something that's real. Maybe that comes from him reading so many books."

"Shoot," Josh said, "I see what you're doing here. This whole project with Kelsey isn't about Kelsey. This is about Justin! This is why you pushed them together. You're hoping Kelsey will defibrillate Justin from his messed up perspective."

Drew grinned and said, "Well if any chick can defibrillate a guy, it would be Kelsey."

"So after a couple of days, Justin mustered up the courage to go talk to this girl again and he asked her out." Drew and Josh stopped in their tracks. They smiled as they both looked over at Adam with bated breath. "She rejected him! She completely flipped out on him again."

"Good grief," Josh said, waving his hand.

"Are they talking now?" Drew asked.

"I don't know. I doubt it. We can probably assume they haven't even been eating lunch together anymore."

As they quietly finished playing the sixth hole, the breeze picked up and a cumulus cloud moved in front of the sun. They ambled toward the path through the trees leading to the tee for the seventh hole, but Josh suddenly stopped. "Whoa," he said as he grasped for Adam's shirt to hold him still.

"What?" Adam asked. Drew turned and looked in the same direction. It was a mountain lion, creeping along about a hundred and fifty feet away on the hillside to the north. Adam warily began to step back.

"Don't do that," Josh whispered. "We're good. He's not going to mess with us." The mountain lion sighted them but was indeed more scared of them, three larger figures standing together. Josh grabbed his camera and feverishly attached his zoom lens as Adam and Drew watched the cougar scurry up the hillside. Josh rapidly took five pictures, but the cat disappeared over the hill to the northwest, away from the course. "We're alright," Josh said. "There have been several reports of mountain lion sightings in that Silver Springs development down the hill there."

"Did you get any good shots?" Adam asked.

"Nah, I'm coming back though."

They continued with their round, getting separated on each hole as they searched through the trees and sagebrush for their discs. Rumblings of thunder could still be heard occasionally off to the west but the sky remained clear overhead. When they approached the shorter thirteenth hole, there were two other parties ahead of them waiting to tee off. Adam, Josh, and Drew held back, about forty feet behind the tee. Despite the storms in the distance, it was a pleasant evening and they were perfectly content to relax and watch others play. The hole was free of any trees and one of the prime locations on the course for a potential hole-in-one.

"So are the Buckeyes going to win it all this year?" Drew asked.

Adam shrugged as Josh replied with a high pitch squeal, "Heck yeah."

"Ah, they got so screwed last year. I tell you, the current college football playoff system is unmitigated disaster."

"Alright," Adam gushed, "here's what they need to do." Josh rolled his eyes as he looked over at Drew. "Twelve teams," Adam said. "Automatic bids would of course go to the champions of the five power conferences, the ACC, the Big Ten, the Big 12, the Pac-12, and the SEC, and automatic bids would also go to the champions of the five other conferences, the mid-majors or whatever you call them, but only if those champions finish with a ranking in the top twenty. At-large bids would be given to two additional teams, or more if additional spots are available due to a mid-major champion not finishing with a ranking in the top twenty."

"What ranking?" Josh asked.

"An established selection committee of experts would be specifically created to rank the top twenty-five teams in the football bowl subdivision. The rankings would also be referenced to set the early matchups." Adam started pacing as he continued, "Okay, so the four highest ranking teams in the tournament would get a bye. Four initial games would take place a week or so before Christmas. Four follow up games would take place after Christmas, and the two semifinal games would occur around New Year's Day. A final championship game would occur a week later." Adam looked at Drew, and with his hands out and palms up, he said, "There you go." Adam grinned and yelled, "Oh my gosh, can you imagine?"

"It's not going to happen," Josh said.

"Well, if I was elected President," Adam replied, "on my first day in office, I would issue an executive order to assure the college football playoff system was changed to such a system and every American would be happy."

"Under what authorization?" Drew asked. "What law would give you, as President, the authority to issue such an executive order?"

"I guess I would have to get my lawyers to work on that, but I'm sure there's an existing law that would give the President such authority. The order would probably be legal as part of oversight of federal funding that goes to universities and athletic departments." Drew scoffed as Adam giggled gleefully.

"I'm telling you," Drew said, "the Bowls would sue and go all the way to the Supreme Court if necessary to halt any progress toward your perfect college football tournament."

"No, they would be fine. The Bowls would be part of it. Bigger, more established Bowls, would serve as games for earlier rounds in the tournament. Other Bowls would still be important as post-season options for the teams that don't make the tournament. Historical inter-conference rivalries would be preserved as much as possible."

"Not going to happen," Drew said.

"Look, the NCAA has failed," Adam whined. "They've failed the fans, they've failed the coaches, and they've failed the student athletes. The current playoff system is an affront to college football fans everywhere. The NCAA has failed to provide coaches with an adequate and appropriate system for determining a true National Champion, and as for the athletes, the players have always done their job, but until the NCAA converts to such an appropriate playoff system, the NCAA has failed every player that works so hard at becoming a model athlete and a model student."

"I'm sorry, but it's not going to happen," Josh said, concurring with Drew.

Adam started kicking at the dirt. "It would be so perfect," he mumbled.

As Adam sulked, Josh and Drew watched a group of three kids throw their tee shots. All their shots landed near the thirteenth basket. They scrambled up the slope to their discs, but another couple was also waiting, so Drew stepped to his left and sat on a large rock. Josh followed his lead and sat on a log to Drew's right.

Adam gazed off at the dark clouds to the west that were moving farther south. "Why do things have to get so messed up?" he asked. "The current college football playoff system is like the Internal Revenue Code. Everyone knows there's a better way, but it doesn't get fixed. And we have to live with it. It's the same deal with Kelsey. There are all these extraneous, outside forces that cause her situation to be so messed up, but none of it should have ever happened." Adam tilted his head as the sun suddenly shined bright through a cloud. He looked back at Drew and asked, "What if I have a daughter some day?"

Drew jerked his head up. He held his hand over his sunglasses and looked at Adam for a couple seconds. "The Webbs are real conservative," Drew said. "I met her parents a couple times when they were in town and stopped by to see her at one of our work sites. She's also talked about them a bunch. My understanding is that they were very strict when they raised her. In high school, she didn't get to go out on dates. She didn't get exposed to much at all. It sounds like we wouldn't even recognize that version of Ms. Webb. But when she got free of their shackles, boy, she went wild."

"How many wet t-shirt contests has she won?" Josh asked.

Drew turned, wiggled his eyebrows, and replied, "I can tell you this, if she enters, she'll win."

"I think there's a similar problem even now," Adam said. "Her parents see the solution as locking her up in her old bedroom down in Lubbock. That's not going to do anything to fix the source of her problem."

"You know," Drew said, "I have an eight-year-old daughter. When I see Ms. Webb and the way she's living her life, I do think about my daughter so much. My daughter is so beautiful, and some day, I'm going to have to protect her …from dudes like me!"

"Nah," Josh said, "you never hurt anyone. Kelsey didn't get into such a state from hanging out with guys like you."

"I'll tell you," Drew said, "I'm going to be so blunt and so direct when I talk to my daughter about the bad boys and the hot boys–"

"And the older boys," Adam interjected.

"Yeah," Drew continued, "and how she has to be vigilant of all of them. I'm going make sure she knows that while I understand and acknowledge the tendencies to have fun and revel in rebellion, it won't be an option under my watch."

"Don't wait till she's seventeen," Josh said. "It's way too late then."

"How do you do it?" Adam asked. "How do you impart to your kids that they have an opportunity to have fun while they're young, and that's fine, but they also need to seize the opportunity to make their life extraordinary and make smart decisions, every day, in every aspect of their life."

"Be there," Drew said, "from the beginning. I work too much, but I'm so lucky. Amy's so good with them. She loves it so much, and she wants to do it."

They quietened as the couple in front of them shuffled around and prepared to throw their tee shots. They both winged forehands, their discs falling off to the right.

"I don't know," Adam said as the couple began walking briskly toward their discs.

"Adam," Drew interjected, "you would be fine. You would be such a great dad. Hannah would be an awesome mother." Drew laughed as he turned to Josh. "You know, my daughter is more scared of Amy than me. It's funny, it works every time. All I have to do is threaten, 'Do you want to me go get your mother?', and boy, does my daughter jump."

"I might be a little scared of Amy myself," Adam said.

"You better be," Drew replied with chuckle.

Drew and Josh stood up and watched the couple in front of them as they moved swiftly toward their discs. They quickly zinged their second shots up close to the basket. "It really is up to Ms. Webb to get it sorted out," Drew said. "I will say I'm liking your plan with Mr. Hayes more and more. Maybe he can get through to her in a way that nobody else could and get her to change her perspective."

"Heck, I'm now more curious to see what happens to Justin," Josh said. "He is one tough nut to crack."

"Alright," Drew said, twirling his disc on his finger, "what's the score? I know I'm out, but I'll enjoy following your competition."

"Adam's up by two strokes," Josh said.

"Did Hayes really describe uranium enrichment to Ms. Webb?" Drew asked. Adam and Drew busted out laughing as they nodded. "What's next?" Drew asked.

"We're going with your idea," Adam responded. "The gold standard."

After waiting a few more seconds for the group in front of them to clear the basket, Adam suddenly yelled, "Damnit, I want a twelve team college football tournament!"

Chapter 7 – Tarnished Gold on the Pool Table

With the persistent rain that Thursday evening, it was chilly enough that Jake, the owner of the North Fork Tavern, had a fire blazing in the wood stove and most of the windows were sealed. Outdoor activities in the Spruce Creek valley were washed out, so the joint was hopping and tunes were playing louder than normal. Adam, Hannah, Josh, and Emily had arrived together and each were seated at their usual spots at their usual table, the high top along the windows and opposite the bar. They were all dressed nicely having arrived from work. Justin, certainly aware of their presence, was already seated in his normal spot as he perused the latest edition of the Spruce Creek News and chowed down on his food order. Kelsey was also there. She was shabbily dressed and standing at the bar with her boys, and while she was smiling, her spirit was calmer than normal.

"It is quite amazing," Josh said, resuming their conversation about the business at his gallery. "We made more than forty percent of our annual revenues during the holidays last year. We could have done better if I had been more prepared, had more product ready, and stayed open later."

"Wow," Adam mumbled as he looked out the window that was opaque with condensation. Hannah had cracked the window open enough so Cody could hear their voices. She lowered her head to peer through a small clear circle in the fogged up window, and Cody had finally lay down on the covered walk. The rain was heavy and noisy as it pounded the parking lot, but Cody wasn't the type of canine to be affected by the rain or the rumbles of thunder and flashes of lightning. Hannah and Adam knew Cody would sure rather be there than home alone.

"But explain this to me," Josh continued, talking with elevated volume to be heard over the chatter in the tavern, "it's been over two thousand years since the birth of Jesus Christ, right? People are still celebrating his birth. But they celebrate it primarily by spending money."

"Are you complaining?" Adam asked.

"No, but think about it. As a result, businesses have a keen interest in seeing the celebration of Jesus Christ's birthday perpetuated forever. It significantly alters their bottom line, and it's in their own personal interest to see the celebration sustained. It greatly influences the amount of wealth they can amass."

"Josh," Hannah grumbled, "I don't want to hear any of this pagan talk tonight."

"I don't have a problem with the general idea," Josh went on, looking at Adam. "Even though we have little clue regarding the actual date that Jesus was born, it makes sense that in December, during the darkest, coldest time of year, people would seize the opportunity to take a break from school or their jobs, spend more time with family and friends, and fatten up for the winter. I get all that, but all the gift giving and the spending will never cease to fascinate me. People use Jesus Christ's birthday, or the date we're going with, as a means to justify spending. They reference Jesus Christ's birthday as a way to make themselves feel better about spending money that they don't have!"

"Are you complaining?" Adam yelled just before a large clap of thunder startled several patrons. Hannah peered out the window again at Cody. The thunder caused him to raise his head, but he lay quietly.

"No," Josh croaked, "heck, I'm going to take full advantage of the situation like all the other corporations and businesses out there profiting off the delusional behavior–"

"Josh!" Hannah yelled.

"But I'll never understand it. Also, is there any interest in discussing the true meaning that Jesus serves in individuals lives or deconstructing the meaning behind biblical parables. No! Everyone is too focused on trying to see that their own personal social agenda is forced on the rest of the country and the rest of the world."

"Josh!" Hannah screamed. Notwithstanding all the background noise in the astir environment that evening, Hannah's screams startled the family at an adjacent table.

"Okay, okay," Josh yammered, "I'll stop." He looked down and smiled as he mumbled, "Now that's some righteous indignation."

"Josh!" Hannah protested again.

"Hey," Emily said, looking at Josh, "I can do a bunch of framing in October. Seriously, have the pictures ready and frames ordered and I'll crank out some framing for you. We'll make sure the gallery is ready for the holidays this year."

"What's your best seller these days?" Adam asked.

Josh started chuckling as he replied, "After all the exploring I've done, heading out at the crack of dawn, three days a week, hiking up Wallace Gulch, driving up and over Willow Pass, or parking my butt in the middle of the refuge for hours and hours, my best seller is that photo I took of the bull moose in the wetlands right outside my condo."

"Yeah, yeah," Adam said, "where it's pouring down rain but the rays from the sun are shining through the clouds."

Josh nodded affirmatively. A server walked up to the table with a pitcher for Adam and Josh, Emily's signature mixed drink, and an ice water for Hannah. "I'm going to find that mountain lion tomorrow," Josh said, lightly pounding his fist on the table.

"Josh," Emily yelled.

"Oh Emily, that cougar won't want to have anything to do with me. It will probably run up a tree as soon as it sees me."

"Take Cody with you," Hannah said. Cody raised his head after he hearing his name and looked up at the window. "Cody would love it," Hannah said, sprightly. "He'll chase that cat up a tree for you."

"Hannah," Emily said, "you're not helping." Emily exhaled, turned her head toward Josh, and looked at him in disappointment. He gritted his teeth and patted her on the shoulder.

A loud pop of thunder clapped again, distracting everyone. Emily slowly looked around the crowded scene at the tavern and waved at a couple of locals. As Josh and Adam focused on the Rockies baseball game broadcast on all the televisions, Hannah whipped her head around and looked at Kelsey. Kelsey was still standing with her boys, but her demeanor remained noticeably subdued. Hannah slowly leaned her head on Adam's shoulder as she watched Kelsey. Adam reached his arm around her and rubbed her back gently. After a minute, Kelsey made eye contact with Hannah, and Hannah quickly looked away. Kelsey trudged over.

"Hi," Hannah said, getting up to give Kelsey a hug. "Look at you, all showered and dolled up. What's the occasion?" Kelsey shrugged as she looked down to survey her attire, a brand new, bright red top and some tight, black jeans. "Hey," Hannah said with her arm still around Kelsey's shoulders, "the gents are going to the Rockies game tomorrow night so Emily and I doing happy hour at the gallery. You should stop by."

"What time?" Kelsey asked as Hannah released her embrace.

"We won't close the gallery until 8:00, so whenever." Kelsey responded with a dispassionate shrug. "Well," Hannah added, "we'll be there." Hannah walked back around to her seat and then looked at Josh as she said, "We should go on another hike or something."

"Just tell me where to be," Josh said.

Adam looked at Kelsey and asked, "Do you have a bike?"

"Nope. I used to, but I left it at Brandon's."

"I could borrow a bike from Jessica," Hannah said.

"I wouldn't expect that Justin would want to ride any single track," Josh said. "Let's ride the forest service road up to Riley Ridge. How about Saturday?" Everyone nodded slowly.

Hannah looked at Kelsey and asked, "Will you ask Justin?" Kelsey looked over at Justin who had taken the last bite of his food order. "Hey," Hannah said as Kelsey turned back, "play a game of pool with him."

Adam pulled some quarters out of his pocket and smacked them on the table. "Here," he said with a nod. Kelsey's shoulders slouched.

"Please," Hannah said, "come on, look at the kid over there." Kelsey begrudgingly looked over and sighed as she turned back toward Hannah. "I know," Hannah added. "Look, Emily and I got a good dose of Justin at the Java Alley on Tuesday. Trust me, we understand your misgivings, but please do it."

"The gold standard," Adam said.

"What?" Kelsey screamed, her eyes narrowing.

"Ask him to explain the gold standard to you."

Following an acrid exhale, Kelsey slapped her hand on the table to grab the quarters and trudged over toward Justin.

Justin was engrossed in a longer Associated Press article in the newspaper and didn't notice Kelsey at first. "Get up," she said, "I'm going to kick your butt in pool." Several others in the tavern leered at Kelsey as she proceeded to the pool table. She squatted at the side of the table, inserted the quarters, and slammed the coin slot. Even with the numerous conversations and classic rock playing through multiple speakers, the bellow of the pool balls dropping under the table and the subsequent rattle of the balls running on the tracks to the ball return distracted several of the patrons.

As Justin moseyed over to the table, Kelsey was assertive as she racked the balls and grabbed a pool cue off the wall. "You break," she said abruptly. Justin sluggishly grabbed a cue and lined up for his break. With a spark of energy, he released an absolute sledgehammer break. The sound of the balls banging against each other resounded throughout the tavern. Kelsey's hazel eyes danced as she watched the balls ricochet off the rails. Two balls sank in a corner pocket. "Ah," Kelsey said, "I see how you are." Justin summarily knocked in three more balls. "I wouldn't have guessed," Kelsey responded, nodding her head playfully.

"It's all about the angles, conservation of momentum, and the coefficient of restitution between the balls and the rails."

Kelsey quipped, "I'm already guessing that I'm going to need some restitution for having to participate in this conversation." Justin smiled. His heart clearly quivered over Kelsey's witticism and he promptly shanked his next shot. Kelsey stepped up to the table and was deft as she ran out the table with dogged determination. Justin grimaced, stormed around the table, and inserted more quarters for another game. The balls clanked again as they dropped under the table and ran along the tracks. As he grabbed the triangle and kneeled down to grab the balls from the ball return, Kelsey said, "Alright," chalking up her pool cue, "explain the gold standard to me, but Justin, please be succinct. Keep it lucid."

Justin, still kneeling, froze with two pool balls in his hand. He dropped his head and smiled before he peered over at Adam. Adam, Hannah, Josh, and Emily were of course watching intently. "Well, I know it wasn't Josh who suggested this topic," Justin said as he stood up. He finished racking the balls and slammed the triangle in the slot at the end of the table. He paused as he stood, pensive, staring at the perfectly racked triangle of pool balls. Kelsey plodded over to him and leaned back against the end of the table. Justin pivoted and leaned against the table too. Kelsey shifted her body over and pressed up against him.

"You look nice tonight," Justin said, with an inquisitive deflection in his voice, but Kelsey didn't respond. Justin hesitated a few seconds and then mumbled, "Wow, the gold standard." Kelsey's face was a few inches from his. Her eyes rested on him as he started, "Okay, so of course you know that hundreds of years ago, goods were acquired through bartering. If somebody had apples and needed milk, they would look for somebody who had milk and needed apples." Kelsey inhaled, blinked her eyes, and nodded as she slouched back. "Well, that was obviously horribly inefficient. It was inevitable that people would seek out some particular item that could be stored and stockpiled to barter with later. So, you ended up with some sort of commodity money, say, salt or tobacco or beaver pelts."

"Oh," Kelsey purred, "those poor little beavers. Hey, maybe we'll see some beavers on our bike ride on Saturday, up Riley Creek."

"Saturday?"

"Uh, yeah," Kelsey said as she shifted closer to him, "you're riding up Riley Ridge with us on Saturday."

"Okay," Justin replied, his voice cracking. "Anyway, so, as people assessed a good option to use as commodity money, it made sense that precious metals would be used. A key advantage being that governments could mint coins from gold and silver for their societies."

"Who's to say gold has value?"

"Ah, that's interesting, now, isn't it?" Justin looked down at Kelsey's hands and instantly became focused on her calluses. She quickly tucked her hands under her arms. "Gold," Justin went on, "is pretty with its luster and it's rare, but oddly, the value we give it is largely psychological. People simply give gold value. The limited supply is of course key." Kelsey began to lightly play footsie with him. He was wearing his casual dress shoes he wears to work and she was wearing some old but clean lightweight, hiking boots. "Your question is actually perfect," Justin continued. "When governments minted gold or silver coins, the value may have been set to match the market value for the gold or silver in the coin. The coins could be melted down and have the same value as the value of the identical amount of precious metal on the market, but governments could also establish currency by minting coins, or notes and state that the notes have value. That's called fiat money."

"Oh, my roommate, Sadie, drives a Fiat."

"Is she Catholic?"

"No. She's Jewish."

"Actually, I could have guessed that," Justin said, nodding.

"How?"

"The name: Sadie Halper." Justin stood up a bit. "So notes were issued by governments, where in and of themselves, the notes of course did not have value since the notes are simply pieces of paper minted in a manner that could not be duplicated. Well, at least, the goal was that they couldn't be duplicated. The notes had value because the government decreed the notes as money and promised to always exchange gold in return for the notes." Kelsey yawned as she stopped moving her feet and looked up at a television tuned to the Rockies game. "The governments," Justin went on, "then had to keep an adequate amount of gold in supply to exchange for all the issued notes."

"Wait, wait, wait" Kelsey said, standing up off the table. She dubiously stated, "if they're being truthful, governments would have to maintain a mountain of gold, in some vault or wherever, ready to exchange for all those issued notes and coins."

"Exactly," Justin replied with a firm head nod. "You've isolated one aspect of being on the gold standard that, if I may say, tarnishes the whole notion of reinstituting the gold standard. An enormous supply of gold would be needed to back all the U.S. dollars in circulation."

"Wow."

"There are much bigger issues though. First, as a society grows, the population grows, the economy grows, and an increase in the money supply is ideally needed to go along with that growth. With currency tied to a gold standard, the money supply is tied to the amount of gold. As gold is mined, the supply increases, but that change in supply may not be able to keep up with the need for a growing economy. Also, the money supply would be tied to the amount of gold mined in other countries, which poses another problem for the U.S. if the U.S. doesn't have the best relations with the countries that lead the world in mining gold."

"Hey, is gold still mined in Colorado?"

"Sure," Justin replied, "but assume for a moment we have a set amount of gold. With a growing population, we would then have downward pressure on prices for things. That's bad, very bad.

People would hoard money knowing that they would eventually be able to buy products for less money if they waited for prices to fall further. That deflationary process builds on itself, restricting economic growth. A steady, slight amount of inflation is important to keep people spending and the economy chugging."

"So, U.S. dollars are not tied to gold now?"

"No, and without a gold standard, the Federal Reserve can add money to the money supply during economic downturns to encourage economic growth and fight deflation. They don't actually print dollar bills. They buy government securities off the market or they buy securities comprised of mortgages from private institutions. You've probably heard of quantitative easing." Kelsey unleashed a big yawn and nodded lightly. "Those financial institutions that sell those securities to the Fed then have more money to lend. Through such loans, the Fed effectively puts more cash into the economy. That stimulates the economy. This action can trigger inflation though, so it has to be done delicately. When the economy gets too hot, the Federal Reserve will sell securities, effectively pulling cash out of the money supply, which will help to control economic growth and control inflation. Too much inflation is very bad."

Kelsey, stood up, turned around. Her hair fell over her cheeks as she tapped her pool cue on the floor. "Alright, alright, so who's to say dollars have value if it's not tied to gold?"

"What else would you want?"

"I don't know. Justin, you're killing me here. Just tell me."

"Here's the deal. The U.S. has, and will continue to have, a vibrant, strong economy, so U.S. dollars will continue to maintain value. Within the U.S. economy, things of value are created that can be purchased with dollars; therefore, U.S. dollars have value. In fact, other countries are so confident in the value of the U.S. dollar that they tie the value of their currencies to the U.S. dollar."

"Alright, so why would anyone want to go back to a gold standard?"

Justin shook his head and slowly said, "I have no idea. With a gold standard, there would be no wherewithal for the Fed to add money to the money supply during the next downturn in the economy. Essentially every economist in the nation would tell you that it would be asinine for the U.S. dollar to be tied to a supply of gold. As soon as the economy started to go sour, the government would inevitably pull off the gold standard so they could stimulate the economy. Philosophically, it sounds good within a conservative ideology: less government intervention is always good, right? Also, there is fear that the Fed will mess up with their tinkering with the money supply and cause hyperinflation, but removing the option for the central bank to control the money supply is really not an option given everything we now know about macroeconomics. Being on the gold standard previously, decades ago, has been widely considered as a key contributor to the Great Depression."

Kelsey looked up toward the ceiling and yelled, "Adam!" She looked back at Justin. "Why the heck did he want me to ask you about this?"

"I don't know. As with climate change and uranium enrichment, there's certainly a political component to the topic. Banks significantly contribute to political campaigns and they would love to see the gold standard reinstituted because they don't want any inflation. Inflation reduces the value of their loans." Justin stood up. "Kelsey, I despise the politics. I would rather be flayed alive than get into the politics. Ask Adam and Josh to explain the politics." Kelsey opened her eyes wide and shook her head vigorously. "Ask your boss, Drew. He's probably the one that wanted us to discuss this topic." Kelsey shook her head again. "The key point is that without the gold standard, the Fed can now control the money supply much more easily and has much greater control over booms and busts that would otherwise devastate the economy and the lives of all Americans."

One of Kelsey's boys suddenly marched up behind them. With a reproachful look, he yelled, "Kelsey! What the hell are you doing? Why are you talking to this dork again?" Justin whipped around, and with a deeply contemptuous look on his face, Justin stared back at the boy. As the scowl dropped further over Justin's face, he instinctively pulled his shoulders back.

Adam, Hannah, Josh, and Emily were all still watching closely. "Oh Adam," Hannah said.

The boy tugged at Kelsey's red top. Justin gritted his teeth, and with white-hot fervor, he raised his pool cue and slammed it over his knee. "Whoa! Whoa!" Adam yelled as he hopped up and scurried over. Josh was right behind him. The pool cue splintered in two pieces. Thunder happened to be rumbling at the moment Justin broke his cue, and with the music and loud conversations, most patrons didn't notice except for a couple seated adjacent to the pool table. The couple was frozen as they focused on the broken cue and Justin. Justin was now flush and breathing heavily through his teeth as he stared at the boy.

Kelsey smiled and tittered. She pushed her boy back. "Come on, let's go." The boy pointed at Justin as she pushed him away.

Adam raced up to Justin. "Easy, big fella," he said. "Come on, let's go outside for bit." Justin, with a surly look still hardened on his face, pushed against Adam. As Josh scampered up, he was tensely looking around for the tavern owner, but Jake was in the kitchen and had missed the entire exchange. Josh noticed the two servers were aware of the incident and focused on Justin. "Justin," Adam said. Justin was still staring at Kelsey's boy as they walked back to the bar. "Justin, I need your help. I need your help right now. I'm worried about the zebra and quagga mussels out at Lake Labash. You have to help me with this."

Justin turned his head and narrowed his eyes at Adam. "Adam, only veligers have been detected. Larvae. Lake Labash is going to be fine."

"Okay," Adam replied whimsically as he moved toward the door, pulling lightly on Justin's shirt, "but it could be bad, right?"

"Well, yeah," Justin said as he hobbled along with Adam, "I mean, if they don't keep an eye out for it and inspect the boats, the mussels could spread and damage all the infrastructure and the water quality, the entire ecosystem for that matter, and wreck all the recreational options." As they kept stumbling toward the door, Josh managed to get Justin to release his tight grip on the two pieces of pool cue. Josh scurried back over to the pool table and laid the pieces of pool cue under the table. As he chased back after Adam and Justin, he looked at the servers and slowly put his index finger over his mouth.

As Adam, Justin, and Josh stepped outside to the covered walk, Cody's excitement was unabated and Josh went over to calm him. It was still raining heavily and low clouds were shrouding the ski runs and peaks on the ridge across the highway. The gloomy weather seemed to work well to calm Justin's nerves. "You owe Jake a pool cue," Adam said. Justin didn't respond as he stared through the window at Kelsey's boy. "Hey," Adam said, "don't worry about it. Do you really give a flip about those boys?"

Justin looked back at Adam and firmly stated, "I'm all in. Alright? Adam, I will do anything it takes to get Kelsey away from those boys. You just tell me what we need to do."

"Wow, I've never seen you so riled up."

Kelsey's neighbor, Kyle, suddenly came storming through the door. He was wearing clean, light-weight work boots and a thick, plaid, button-down flannel tucked into his rugged work jeans. He had thick, coarse, sandy, short hair and was also endowed with a full but groomed beard over his strong jawline. He was an imposing presence at six feet-three inches tall and a lean, two hundred and ten pounds. He stared at Justin for a couple seconds before saying, "Adam, are you sure you know what you're doing here?" Kyle took a couple steps toward Justin. "Are you sure this guy doesn't have any latent maniacal tendencies?"

"Uh, yeah, he's fine," Adam replied.

Distinctly seething, Kyle took another step toward Justin and grunted, "You will rue the day you ever hurt her. I'll break you over my knee. You'll wish you had it as easy as that pool cue." Justin, wide-eyed and shuddering, nodded enthusiastically as he nudged his glasses up on his nose. The glint of the flat, evening daylight reflected off Justin's spectacles as he quivered anxiously. Kyle slowly rotated toward Adam, and Justin finally took a breath. "Also, Adam," Kyle said, "you need to stop calling her crazy."

"What?"

"That Crazy Kelsey stuff has to stop."

"Okay, yeah, sure." Kyle slowly stepped back toward the door and stared back at Justin one last time before going inside.

"Wow," Josh muttered, "he's usually so placid. I can't remember ever seeing him so ornery." Josh looked down at the sidewalk and softly said to himself, "Three people are worked up here like I've never seen them before." He chortled and added, "Well, I guess that's the effect Kelsey has on people."

"Latent maniacal tendencies?" Justin mumbled. "Did he really just say that?" Josh shook his head and waved his hand at Justin. "Do you know what I don't get about that?" Justin continued. "Just because I'm quiet, doesn't mean I'm sine sort of psychopath. I would never hurt a bug." He plopped down on the left side of a bench that was situated against the windows to the tavern. Adam stepped over and sat on the other side. Adam's thoughts had drifted as he stared blankly out at the parking lot. "A sociopath?" Justin went on, "Josh, that's someone that can inflict some serious harm and commit unbelievable atrocities while causing them no distress whatsoever. Gosh, some people are simply shy. It doesn't mean they're sociopaths!" Josh couldn't help but respond with a dry chuckle. "Josh, it's not even social anxiety. Being an introvert is not a disorder."

"It's all good," Josh said. "Don't worry about it."

Justin scoffed. He looked over at Cody who was sitting still but clearly anxious. Above Cody, two hummingbirds were resting on a feeder. The birds were fully resolved to stay in the dry despite the disruption around them. "Actually," Justin said, "I think I know what's going on with Kyle, but it's still laughable. As if I could hurt Kelsey. Kelsey would kick my ass." Josh laughed but Adam was still stoic.

Josh looked at Adam and asked, "What's up?"

"Why have I been calling her crazy?"

"What?"

"Crazy Kelsey. I can't believe I've been saying that. Am I really just now realizing that that's one of the meanest things I've ever done in my entire life?"

"You didn't start it. Heck, everyone in the valley calls her that."

"I've never gotten the impression she likes it," Justin chimed in softly. "I've certainly never seen her respond to it."

Adam shook his head. "Oh my gosh," he whispered. He raised his hands to his head as he sat back. "I'm all in too. Whatever it takes. We're going to fix this. Okay guys?"

Josh leaned against a post and they all relaxed for several seconds before Kelsey stumbled out loudly with her boys. Her boys were gabbing over each other as they tramped by without acknowledging Adam, Josh, or Justin. As they moved past Cody, Cody let out a booming, vicious bark, but Kelsey's boys were unaffected. They ran out into the rain toward their car, but Kelsey turned and walked back toward Justin. She leaned down in front of him and gazed dreamily into his eyes as she rubbed her hand on his chest and down his arm. "You okay?" she whispered. He shrugged. "Don't worry about it. We'll talk more on the bike ride, okay?" He nodded nervously and she scurried back out into the rain after her boys who were waiting in an older, American-made sedan. She squealed excitedly as she hopped in the car.

"So how did it go?" Josh asked. "You get her squared away on the gold standard."

"I guess so," Justin replied.

Josh looked over at Adam and asked, "What's next?"

Adam inhaled and pursed his lips. He watched the car back out of the parking spot, and then the car lurched forward and almost stalled before racing away.

"Where are they going?" Justin asked.

Josh and Adam both looked over at Justin and rolled their eyes as they shook their heads. "You don't want to know," Josh mumbled. Justin winced as he rubbed his knee where he had broken the pool cue. "Are you still going to be able to ride on Saturday?" Josh asked.

"Yeah, you'll probably have to wait on me again."

"Your fine."

"The Israeli-Palestine conflict," Adam blurted out. "Justin can tell Kelsey all about it on Saturday."

"No, no, no," Justin replied. "That one's yours."

Chapter 7 – Tarnished Gold on the Pool Table

Chapter 8 – Spruce Creek Images Deconstructed

Josh's gallery, Spruce Creek Images, located down the valley from the ski resort in a separate building on the south side of the highway, could be seen easily by drivers heading up the valley. The shop was located at the east end of a small retail complex that included a coffee shop, a prosperous steak house, and a Mexican restaurant. The location was fantastic for drawing in walk-ins, although many visitors never bought anything. The store had twenty feet high walls, and there was a line of high windows on the front wall and the left wall as customers entered. Mount Preston and Higgins Peak could be seen perfectly out the front windows, and through the left windows, three cleared lines on the forested hillside were visible in the distance representing three of the resort's west-facing ski runs.

All the walls in the gallery were decked out with numerous framed pictures. Several paintings by a local artists were displayed on the front wall, to the right of the door, but all the other pictures were photographs taken by Josh, mostly around the Spruce Creek valley. Numerous pictures of beautiful, panoramic, mountain vistas donned the left wall, and the right wall was covered with close-up shots of wildlife including elk, bald eagles, coyotes, mountain goats, Rocky Mountain marmots, pikas, and coyotes. To the left of the main checkout counter, at the back of the store, pictures of relics at old mining settlements were displayed. The photographs represented idyll images of life in the valley during the nineteenth century. Several pictures of the Spruce Creek ski area were on exhibit to the right of the counter, and several more photos, including pictures of the moose that was Josh's best seller, were set up on stands in the middle of the gallery.

Bookshelves in front of the counter were stuffed with publications specific to Colorado, including books on the history of mining in the Spruce Creek valley and guides on trails, wildflowers, and fishing in the state. A small barista station was set up on the left side of the counter for making espressos and cappuccinos, and an assortment of homemade pastries were available that were made by Hannah's close friend, Jessica Murphy.

That Friday evening, Hannah and Emily were seated behind the counter, near the entry to a small back room set up for framing. The room could also be configured as a portrait studio. Emily, wearing tan slacks and a new purple blouse, was sipping on a glass of red wine as Hannah, wearing black pants and a bright red top, slouched comfortably with Cody asleep at her feet.

There were no customers at the moment. It was a cooler evening following the cool front that passed the day before, but the weather was still quite nice which likely contributed to the light foot traffic in the gallery. Music was emanating softly through four speakers placed throughout the gallery. The songs were mostly instrumental, acoustic, guitar pieces and were working well to sedate Hannah and Emily. A musky aroma with hints of berries and pomegranate was potent throughout the shop from three fragrance oil warmers that Hannah had lit hours ago.

"It smells so nice in here," Emily commented.

"Josh can't stand it," Hannah replied.

"What?" Emily yelled. "I'll talk to him."

"No, you don't need to say anything. Actually, he never says a word about it, but I know it bothers him. He does appreciate how it helps with the atmosphere and gets attention from walk-ins. He knows we're trying to make money, so he never says anything."

"Maybe I'll get one of these fragrance oil burners for our house, see how he likes that."

"Do you know that picture of those black footed ferrets he took down south?" Hannah asked. "He sold two of those this week."

"We have that picture in our bathroom at home. I'm still so amazed that those pictures of the sandhill cranes aren't selling. I guess they don't qualify as Spruce Creek images, but he put in so much effort to get those shots, traveling way down south to the refuge down there where the cranes stop during their migration. He got up so early, every day, for several days in a row that week."

"Oh, that shot he got of the flock taking flight right after the sun crested the horizon."

"It's so beautiful. We have it in our bedroom."

"Don't worry, they'll sell."

"Yet he sells those pictures he took in North Park last summer of that massive wildfire. Why would anyone want to buy a picture of a forest on fire?"

"You have to admit that shot he got of the fire crowning at the top of the pines is amazing."

"He got in trouble for getting in there so close for that one," Emily said, chuckling.

Hannah shifted in her seat and asked, "So, how's your work?"

"Oh, it's alright," Emily replied, waving her hand. "So, my favorite picture of Josh's is still that one shot of the aurora borealis he took when we were up in the Yukon."

"Ah," Hannah droned, "I'm still so jealous of that trip you took." Josh and Emily drove from Colorado to Alaska the previous fall, camping every night along the way on the Alaska-Canadian Highway. One night, during their trek up the ALCAN, the northern lights lit up the skies for hours. Josh took hundreds of pictures, but one single shot, without a doubt, proved to be best. "Hey," Hannah blurted out, "maybe we could get Justin to elucidate the aurora borealis to Kelsey."

"I'm sure she would appreciate a diversion from anything political."

Bamboo wind chimes, strategically placed near the front door, rattled lightly as a customer entered. "I'll take this," Emily whispered as she patted Hannah on the knee.

Emily's movement woke Cody, and he stood up. Hannah patted him on the head. Emily spent several minutes walking around the store with the customer, a well-dressed lady, in her fifties, with frizzy, blond hair, several rings on her fingers, and multiple bracelets on each wrist. Hannah, running her fingers around Cody's ear, leaned back and rested her head against the back wall. She closed her eyes as she listened to Emily discuss all the available products and review options for getting custom work prepared. After several minutes of checking out the items in stock, the lady gave Emily a business card, shook her hand, and departed.

"Hannah," Emily cried as she scurried back to the counter. "That was the interior designer working to deck out all the condominiums for that new building being built on the east side of the resort." Cody, unable to ignore the excitement, stood up and nuzzled up to Emily.

"Adam's boss designed that building," Hannah responded enthusiastically.

"It sounds like he's the one that told her about us. All the units are going to be sold fully furnished and she might be interested in a large, bulk deal to buy pictures for all the common areas and every single room in every unit." Hannah gaped as she leaned forward. "There are going to be sixty units in that building," Emily said as she grabbed her wine glass off the counter. "I got her card and told her Josh would call her in the morning."

Hannah was mute and wide eyed before she finally whispered, "Oh my goodness." Emily pushed Cody away as she sat down. They sat speechless for several seconds as Hannah shook her head, marveling over the potential opportunity. "Did you ever figure it would all work out so well?"

"No way," Emily responded. "I was telling Josh every day he was totally crazy for doing this."

"Emily, if that deal comes in, you could probably quit your job and help here."

"I'm so ready for that," Emily muttered. Cody let out a soft whimper and lay back down at Hannah's feet. Emily leaned forward to refill her glass of wine. "How's Adam's work?" she asked.

"He was recently offered the option to become partner in his firm, so that's good news, maybe. The work is steady. He grumbles about all the office nonsense, but he loves designing those homes."

"I kind of wish Kelsey was here now," Emily said, "to help us celebrate. You think she'll show?"

"No," Hannah said, rolling her eyes. "We're not cool enough. Have you thought about Justin's theory anymore?"

"About how she can't stand being alone?"

"Yeah."

Emily inhaled and slowly leaned back. "Oh," she mumbled before taking a sip of wine, "I think it's way more complicated than that. I think it's all related to low self-esteem, which kills me, but I think that's it. How can somebody so beautiful be so insecure? Oh, I begrudge her so much her allure." Emily glared up at the ceiling and shook her head. "I'm sure the way boys have treated her has been a huge factor. They all immediately become so enamored of her, but they're obviously interested in one thing. Hannah, the way boys treat her, when she gets together with them, the way they talk to her, and the way they always try to get her all trashed, it's all had such an effect on her, and it doesn't end there. It's the way all of society treats her. Men and women. That allure is always working for her, twenty-four hours a day, seven days a week. She can't turn it off. She can't make a trip to the grocery store, dressed in sweatpants, without getting a response from everybody."

Hannah snorted and said, "She doesn't even work out."

"After all the attention she gets, she gets no respect for her intelligence and no respect for her work ethic, so she ends up seeking approval by giving in to boys, but afterwards, she feels nothing but shame and guilt, and then she stews later over the way she was treated. It's all built up to where, now, she cracks so easily. Obviously, whatever happened with Brandon last winter was particularly tough. By the way, have you seen him lately?"

"I heard he moved over the pass to the next county. I guess he was probably scared of what Kelsey might do to him. No doubt, he's probably found another victim over there."

Emily hesitated as her thoughts drifted. She looked blankly down at the floor and daydreamed for several seconds before firmly saying, "Brandon is hot though."

"Yep."

"Hannah, it's all so stupid. Kelsey could explain the aurora borealis to us. Oh, I hate her. Hannah, I hate her so much. Guys have never had any interest in trying to get me messed up. Guys have never swooned over me."

"Emily," Hannah said firmly, leaning forward and looking into Emily's eyes, "your life is a dream. Josh loves you so much."

"I know. I know." Emily said, waving her hand. "But Hannah, we have to help Kelsey or I'm going to kill her." Hannah chuckled lightly. "Maybe Adam's right," Emily went on. "Maybe Kelsey's parents didn't help to make it any better. I mean, I know it's not their fault, but I thought about this. I bet they didn't appreciate what she had to deal with and they probably had nothing but a negative reaction to her responses to her environment. That assuredly caused Kelsey to be even more insecure. I guess I don't know, but I've heard Josh talk about her parents. I bet her parents saw all those cool boys and older boys and bad boys, trying to break into their house to get to her, and only responded by blaming Kelsey. I wouldn't be surprised if they tried to lock her up and raise her under some strict, conservative control, and it's no wonder that she went wild as soon as she got free."

"Emily, you pointed this out the other day, we don't really know what it was like."

"No, but I went ahead and thought about it some and can't help but assume."

Hannah reached up for a water bottle she had on the counter. She took a swig and asked, "Did you hear about how Brandon laid down his motorcycle with Kelsey riding on the back?" Emily rolled her eyes, nodded, and then shook her head. "I still don't understand how Kelsey got up from that," Hannah added. "What a harrowing incident, and she dismisses the whole experience. Actually, if you watch her closely, you can still see a slight hitch in her gait from the accident."

"Okay, maybe her parents didn't do anything," Emily said, "but they certainly needed to appreciate that the situation was different, from say the situation with my parents. I wasn't popular. My parents had to help me have a healthy, fun social life. No boys were trying to break into my house to get to me, I can assure you of that. I understand that her parents were extremely religious, right?" Hannah nodded as Emily went on, "Of course that's great, but that environment probably made Kelsey feel even worse over basic mistakes associated with being a normal, playful teen." Emily sighed and mocked, "Josh thinks she didn't play any sports growing up because her parents didn't want her exposed to any associated wild scenes, so she watched a lot of television. We can tell by the way she talks."

"I don't think the details about her upbringing would have mattered," Hannah responded. "She's naturally rebellious. There's no way she could have lived a perfectly chaste lifestyle. She has an innate tendency to be wild." Hannah took a sip of her water and continued, "So her parents didn't believe in her, so what? That's good. Nobody else is going to believe in you in this world until you prove it. It's best when parents don't fill their kids heads with unearned self-confidence. It better prepares a person for the real world when their parents don't believe in them." Hannah noticed Emily was about to drop her wine glass. "Here," Hannah said, grabbing her glass and putting it on the counter.

"I guess," Emily replied. "But not finishing college definitely hurt. On top of everything else, now Kelsey has that to wrestle with every day. We've already learned that she's way too smart and way too good a worker to be a lift operator and out there shoveling dirt all summer for Drew."

"She's lucky to be working for Drew. Nobody else would have stuck with her through this. Emily, you don't even know."

"Know what?"

Hannah shook her head. She whipped her head around and hemmed and hawed. "I only know because Drew talked to Adam. You can't tell anyone."

"What?"

"Oh Emily, after she didn't show up to work for two days in a row earlier this summer, Drew went to her place. He found her alone, all wasted. She was sitting in her living room like a zombie. Drew walked around her place and found some stuff in her bedroom. He told her she had to sober up and show up to work the next morning or he was done with her forever."

"Oh Hannah," Emily purred, knitting her brow.

"Well, thankfully, she showed up, and Drew never said another word to her about it. He never told any of the crew members."

"Hey, did she ever take prescription opioids?"

"Yep, the ski season before last, when she was working as a lift op. She had thrown her back out pulling the chairs back for the El Otro Lado lift, one after another, and got a prescription for one of the opioids for three months. After the season was over, the doctor refused to continue her prescription, ...but she got more."

"Well, if Kelsey wants something, she's not one to have any trouble getting what she wants."

"Yeah, she was able to get more and she kept taking them for months, but it gradually got more difficult for her to find them."

"How's her back now?"

"Oh, her back's fine. You saw her hiking. I'm hoping that's a significant positive factor in all this."

"Anyway, after Drew's ultimatum, she stayed clean for a while, but then, a couple weeks ago, she was at the Spot, late at night, for one of Tyler's deejaying gigs. My friend Jessica saw her there. She was supposedly hopped up on something. Jessica said she was bouncing off the walls and most of the people there were staying away from her."

"Smoking weed?"

"No, no, no, definitely not. I wish that was all it was. That would be fine. Actually, Drew had indicated that access to cannabis really helped her to ween off opioids, but now, ...the problem is those boys."

"Ugh," Emily groaned.

"Anyway, Drew heard about that night at the Spot. I pleaded with him to not do anything yet. I saw her a couple days later outside the Java Alley, and I went up to her and hugged her. Emily, I couldn't let go. I hugged her so tightly, and then I started crying. I was bawling. I couldn't control it. I nuzzled my face into her to try to hide it from the others in the plaza. I refused to let go. She finally squeezed me back. I begged her, Emily. I begged her to stop getting wasted. I was crying my eyes out, and she could barely tell what I was saying, but I told her that she had to stop for me. I told her how I was so worried about her all the time. I hadn't been able to sleep. I hadn't been able to focus at work, and she had to stop. If she hurt herself, she would hurt me. She would hurt a lot of people. I told her that she didn't realize what she was doing to other people."

"What did she say?"

"Nothing at first but she eventually started crying too and hugged me back. Then it was she who wouldn't let go. She finally said, 'Okay,' convincingly. That's when I gave her my phone number and told her to call me whenever she needed me."

"Oh Hannah, please be careful."

"I will, but I'll also say this. People in society have to help each other. She needs help, and Emily, I'm going to help her. We're going to figure this out. If she doesn't get help, then what? Maybe she ends up pregnant or in need of some serious health care with no insurance or in prison. Then what? She's a burden on everyone then, and there's no need for that to happen." Tears welled up in Hannah's eyes. "Or even worse," Hannah started and her lips quivered as she began to sob, "we lose her. We can't lose her, Emily." Hannah reached over to hug Emily.

Emily hugged her back awkwardly given the way they were sitting. "Does Justin know what we're dealing with here?"

"No," Hannah whimpered, pulling back. "Remember when he was asking about Sadie leaving Kelsey alone at their place? I didn't tell him that Kelsey's actions drove Sadie away." Hannah wiped her eyes.

"Oh Hannah, please be careful. Justin's not looking for any trouble. If she rends his heart in two-"

"Here's the thing though, Kelsey would never hurt him. I've been thinking about this a lot, and I've decided that's what's so brilliant about Adam's idea. Pushing him onto her was like giving her a new puppy. Justin's innocence is having such an effect on her. I know she would never do anything to hurt him and she would never expose him to anything that would tarnish his purity. She would never let those boys hurt him. Also, Justin's smart. We can confidently know that he can assess any situation and handle it himself."

"Now I'm curious to know what's going on with you," Emily said, "and why you're doing this. You're usually so shy and demure, but you've gotten yourself into something serious. I know you're as altruistic as anyone and not a save yourself first kind of person, but this is some heavy duty stuff you're dealing with." Emily paused and looked down at Cody. "I guess it's good that you're the one doing this. Kelsey believes in you. She knows you're one person that would never hurt her. She can't trust others because of the way they feel about her and treat her or the way they've treated her in the past. She hasn't received the kind of positive attention you're offering. I know I couldn't do it. I just want to kill her."

"I think Justin's in a better position to help. Have you noticed how he treats her with so much respect?"

"Yeah. You know what I don't get?" Emily asked, chuckling. "Justin's definitely affected by her, but she's not getting to him the way she gets to everyone else."

"He's not gay."

"No, no, no," Emily responded. "Heck, if he doesn't stop staring at my chest, I'm going to slap him sideways one of these days."

Hannah busted out laughing. "Oh, don't do that. He's fine."

"I know, but see, I don't get that either. That's another reason why I want to slap him sideways. So he was a dorky nerd growing up and probably had to start wearing glasses as a child, had braces all through high school, and always had a couple whopper zits every week. I bet his parents are boring, old sticks-in-the-mud. Okay, so he didn't get invited to parties or whatever and became horribly self-conscious about his appearance and transitioned into a wallflower at a young age. So what? He doesn't have any zits now. I do want to give him some shaving advice, but his teeth are straight and I love his hipster glasses. He dresses nice. He's obviously incisive and smart as a whip and has so many endearing qualities. He certainly has some intriguing perspective and profound opinions on major aspects of life."

"Did you know he can play the piano?"

"No!"

"Yeah, he can play ragtime."

"Hannah! Let's kill him. Let's throw him down the glory hole spillway at Labash Dam. That will take care of him."

Hannah chuckled and said, "I hear everything you're saying and you're right, there's something else going on with the guy, but I think he's coming to terms with being a dork. He's too smart not to figure all that out on his own." Hannah nodded gently and said, "But you're right, there's something else going on. We would be remiss not to accept that. We simply don't know what it is yet."

"Kelsey's intrigued too, and I think she wants to figure it out."

"She'll get it out of him."

The bamboo wind chimes rattled as a middle-aged couple stepped into the store. Hannah got up. Emily grabbed Cody's collar and petted him. The couple was dressed casually but was obviously more affluent. They were clearly not interested in talking, so Hannah stayed back as they reviewed all the options for about ten minutes. The woman eventually became captivated by a framed photograph of eight mountain goats that Josh took up on Willow Pass. The picture was taken late in the summer where every mountain goat had already shed its winter coat, and all the beautiful goats were looking right at the camera. They motioned to Hannah, and after a quick exchange, Hannah grabbed the picture off the wall. Emily wrapped it up as Hannah rang up the sale. Hannah and Emily sat back again as the couple departed.

"Okay, so now what?" Hannah asked. Emily, with a quizzical look on her face, looked at Hannah. "It's not as simple as Kelsey not wanting to be alone with her thoughts. Okay, so how does Kelsey beat it?" Emily hemmed and hawed a bit but didn't respond. "What scares me," Hannah said, "is she doesn't care anymore. She doesn't care about what she does or what people think. She doesn't ponder her future for one second. She has no hopes or dreams. She doesn't care about anything. I guess in one sense, there's a certain brilliant beauty to the product you get from her, which of course contributes to why people are so affected by her, but it also feels like what you might see from a brilliant artist before they commit suicide. The signs are there. Emily, I wish she would start going to church."

"Oh, I don't know," Emily responded. "Again, it sounds like she was exposed to plenty of that growing up. Sure, the environment works to get some people where they need to be, but for Kelsey, there may be another more direct and efficient way to successfully get her there. It would probably be easier to focus on the basics. First, she has to fully and categorically renounce those boys. You're sure right about that. Stop hanging out with those dolts. Hang out with some different people. And she has to quit putting herself in positions where she inevitably won't be treated right. She has to stop exposing herself to bad influences. If someone has a problem with candy, they need to stay out of the candy store. And she needs to finish school. School's not even something I'm hung up on, but I do believe it's critical for her. School can beget so many unintended but good consequences." Emily reached down and petted Cody gently as she went on, "Most importantly, she has to come to terms with all the bad memories. She has to become comfortable with her thoughts. Those memories will always be there, at the forefront of her mind. I couldn't even begin to relate, but I know she can do it. She has to live with them. Getting involved with a church may provide a good environment to accomplish all that, but there may be other ways."

"I worry she'll never be able to do it alone."

Emily looked at Hannah and said, "You know what she needs? She needs the right person to come along who will protect her from all the bad influences, be there by her side during the down times, and tactfully encourage her to head down a positive path."

"Sounds like some sort of comic book hero."

.

Chapter 9 – Finances Devalued at the Stadium

A light breeze blew past Adam's ears as he sat, midway up the lower level on the third base side at the Colorado Rockies baseball stadium. He stared toward the left-handed hitter who was up to bat with a three-two count in the bottom of the third inning. Adam's view of the action was almost perfect, and while there was a good crowd on hand that Friday evening, he, along with Josh and Drew, somehow lucked out and were surrounded by several empty seats. With the temperature at eighty-two degrees and fair skies overhead, the entire crowd had become lulled into a sustained state of calm.

Following the two-hour drive from Spruce Creek to Denver, Adam, Josh, and Drew had managed to clear their heads from the hectic goings-on at their workplaces. Adam had a bag of peanuts and was cracking shells, one by one, and popping the nuts into his mouth as he threw the shells at his feet. Josh, to his left, had turned and was watching a small flock of starlings circle over the flag poles in center field and then disappear behind the right field stands. Drew, to Adam's right, with a half-full beverage in hand, had let his thoughts wander as he gazed at the Mets infielders who were standing easy but on their toes as they waited for the next pitch.

As the consistent murmur from a myriad conversations reverberated around the stadium, the pitcher for the New York Metropolitans shook off two signs before he got set to throw from the stretch, with a Rockies runner on first. The tall, lanky, right-handed pitcher with a scruffy beard peered over his shoulder as the runner stared intently back. The runner slowly stepped farther and farther away, and as he got settled with his lead, the pitcher looked over his shoulder yet again before stepping off the rubber and faking a throw, causing the runner to slide back to first.

The hurler wiped some sweat off his forehead, took a deep breath, and stepped against the rubber again. After the catcher dropped his fingers to call for a pitch, the pitcher accepted the first sign, and the hard-throwing ace took one final look over his shoulder before delivering a ninety-four mile per hour fastball that was fouled off toward Adam, Josh, and Drew. Drew jumped out of his seat and almost spilled his beverage, but the ball soared well over his head and into the upper deck.

Drew slowly sat back down and asked, "Is everything still on track with Ms. Webb?"

Adam shrugged and watched the next pitch before responding, "I'm not sure what's going to happen. I've actually been having more fun monitoring Justin's development." Josh chuckled lightly.

"I sure would love to have seen Mr. Hayes go all maniacal on her boys last night," Drew said. "How sweet would that be to watch him take that broken pool cue and beat every one of those boys to a pulp?"

"Ah, he would never do that," Adam said. "Kelsey would break it up and whip all their hides before it came to that." Adam shifted back in his seat. "I'll give Hannah credit. She's making progress."

Josh chimed in, "We're going to ride up Riley Ridge tomorrow."

A roar from the crowd suddenly erupted as the Rockies hitter smacked a laser of a line drive into the right field gap. The runner on first was able to motor all the way around third, the third base coach wheeling his arm around and around. The hitter strolled into second with a stand-up double and pointed toward the sky. Josh, Adam, and Drew were clapping but remained seated as there was nobody directly in front of them to block their view.

"Alright," Adam yelled as he nodded fervently and pumped his fist.

The Rockies shortstop was up to bat next, and with the first pitch, he hit one right up the elevator shaft. The Mets catcher stood up and waited several seconds for the ball to descend before gloving the baseball just a few steps from home plate. That was the end of the third inning. As the public address announcer began chatting about the between-innings entertainment, several members of the crowd started heading up the aisles.

"Did Mr. Hayes get Ms. Webb all straightened out on the gold standard?" Drew asked, turning slightly toward Adam. Adam nodded and smiled, showing his teeth. "Hey," Drew said, "did he also discuss why countries devalue their currencies?"

"I don't think so," Adam replied.

"I would like to hear Mr. Hayes' explain that."

Josh perked up, and with a big grin, he asked, "Can I try?"

Adam popped a couple more peanuts in his mouth. He turned his head toward Josh. Drew turned too before shrilling, "Yeah."

Josh, still smiling, shifted forward in his seat. "Okay," he started, clearing his throat, "so, when countries were on the gold standard, there would effectively be a fixed exchange rate for exchanging the two countries' currencies. The exchange rate would be tied to the amount of gold they each had, right?" Drew and Adam were nodding as they inhaled and twisted a bit more in their seats to face Josh. "A trade imbalance," Josh went on, "between two countries, when under the gold standard, would result in an increase in the money supply for the surplus nation, or an increase in the amount of gold for that nation, followed by an increase in inflation. That would lead to more expensive goods which would subsequently cause a decrease in their exports, right?" Adam nodded slowly. "The deficit nation would see a decrease in their amount of gold which would be followed by deflation. That would lead to less expensive goods which should result in an increase to their exports."

"Okay," Adam chimed in, "so theoretically, with the surplus nation seeing increased inflation and a decrease in exports and the deficit nation seeing deflation and an increase in exports, the natural effect would be a shift back towards a balance in exports and imports between the two countries."

"Yeah, yeah," Josh said. "The problem was that during economic downturns, the nation with a trade deficit would be hit with additional deflationary pressures."

"Hold on," Drew said, "if countries are not on the gold standard but using floating exchange rates, the effect should still be the same though, right? A country with a surplus in exports is going to feel a follow-up positive influence to their economy, inflationary pressure, and increase to prices, and the country with a trade deficit will feel deflationary pressure and a potential decrease in prices."

"Yeah, yeah," Josh replied.

"Just so I understand," Adam said, "an aside here. Without the gold standard, the exchange rates between currencies vary depending on many factors: the two countries' inflation rates, interest rates, trade deficits, operating deficits and debts, prices for exports versus imports, and the stability of the governments."

"Yeah, shut up," Josh said as he smacked Adam's chest with the back of his hand. "Let me try to do this. Okay, getting to Drew's original question and why countries devalue their currencies, even if countries are not working with fixed exchanges rates, there are measures a country can take to devalue their currency and make exports cheaper for the rest of the world and make imports more expensive. A country with a trade surplus could offset the natural negative impact to their exports by expanding their money supply and then buying a foreign currency or using that extra money to expand their domestic economy. Such actions allow a country to stimulate their economy." Josh reached down and grabbed his beverage from a cup holder. "But it can have consequences," he said before he took a sip.

"Well sure," Adam interjected, "it could go so far as to cause soaring inflation, and the citizens of the country get hit. Their wealth is worth less. Also, the country looks weaker in the international community if they implement such measures and their own government debt will be more expensive."

"The sons of bitches are exporting their unemployment to a different country," Drew exclaimed.

"Other countries would likely take action to counter the effect by also devaluing their currencies," Adam said. "Then you have a currency war."

"Damnit," Josh blurted out, "let me do this."

"Sorry," Adam mumbled as he slouched in his seat.

"So consider China," Josh said. Drew shook his head and rolled his eyes as he twisted around to monitor the action on the field. Adam also concentrated on home plate as the top of the fourth inning had begun. Josh hesitated in thought for a moment as he looked down at the pile of peanut shells by Adam's feet. "I can do this," he said softly before inhaling. "So, the U.S. has a trade deficit with China. As a result, there is a greater demand for the Chinese currency, the yuan, and less demand for U.S. dollars." Drew and Adam turned back toward Josh as he continued, "The Chinese currency would then have greater value, pushing up the price for Chinese goods. The effect would theoretically be appropriate in the sense that it would naturally help to balance trade, which is good for the world economy, but if China subsequently implements measures to devalue their currency, to keep prices for their exports cheap and imports expensive, they will maintain their surplus and maintain their trade position."

"Punk ass bitches!" Drew yelled, pounding his fist on his knee.

An older couple, seated three rows in front of him, turned, and with a look of scorn, they stared at Drew. Drew gritted his teeth and looked over at Adam and Josh who both lowered their heads and were trying to suppress their laughter.

Adam leaned forward and whispered, "I believe the International Monetary Fund was created after the Great Depression and World War II with a specific goal of fostering good trade relations and trying to prevent countries from getting into such currency wars."

"Seriously, did I get all that right?" Josh asked

"I think so," Adam replied. Drew nodded.

Josh crossed his arms, tipped his head up, and cracked a sardonic smile. "Not bad for a nature photographer, eh?"

They focused on the game for the next couple innings with little conversation and became somewhat despondent as the Mets rallied for five runs in the top of the fifth inning to go up six to two, but being long-time Rockies fans, they were resigned to the notion that a loss is always possible. The weather remained fair, and while it was warm, it was cooler than normal for a mid-summer night in Denver. As the bottom of the sixth inning began, Drew finally returned from the concessions with a hot dog and a second beverage. Josh had taken out his camera and zoom lens and was taking photos of players and numerous other scenes from around the stadium. The Rockies catcher led off the bottom of the sixth with a slow ground ball to the Mets shortstop.

Drew shook his head and said, "I don't know how you baseball dorks can stand watching this stuff all the time." Adam and Josh were expressionless as they gazed at the Mets pitcher who had only given up three hits so far. "What are the chances we'll see somebody try to steal home tonight?"

"Zero," Adam summarily replied.

"Well," Drew said, "teach me something here. What's a Silver Slugger again?"

"Silver slugger awards are presented at the end of each season," Adam responded, "to the best offensive player at each position. Separate awards are given out for the National League and American League, as voted on by coaches and managers."

"And Gold Gloves?"

"Those are given every year to the best fielding players at each position," Josh said, stowing his camera.

"Again, as voted on by coaches and managers," Adam added.

"Ugh," Drew grunted before taking a bite of his hot dog. "I would rather talk politics." Drew gave a light, backhanded smack to Adam's chest. "So when's this grand plan of yours going to happen?"

Adam sighed and rolled his eyes as Josh chuckled. "Not until we see some serious campaign finance reform," Adam muttered.

Adam, Josh, and Drew made politics a regular topic of discussion for many years, but Adam was generally the crusader looking to incite the debates. Prior to the last Presidential election, Adam insisted on formulating a starting point for implementing lasting solutions to all the key issues of the day, social security, health care, discretionary spending, and education among other topics, all to put an end to the years of political tumult and prepare the country for the new challenges of the twenty-first century. This grand plan, as he called it, didn't pass muster with Josh and Drew and certainly had not been an area of focus for the latest Congress.

"Now there's a topic for your egghead, Mr. Hayes," Drew said. "We need to get him to explain the issues with getting campaign finance reform implemented."

"No, he wouldn't like that," Adam replied. "I'm telling you, he loves the science and the technical aspects of issues, but he abhors the politics. Plus, the current approach to campaign financing is so ineffectual that I doubt Justin could even bear to discuss it."

"Oh, let me try," Josh blurted out. "I want to try this one too."

Drew and Adam grinned as they looked at each other before simultaneously turning their heads toward Josh. "Alright, go for it," Drew said.

"Okay," Josh started, shifting forward to the edge of his seat, "so let's start back in the 1970s when Congress first passed a law, that was subsequently tweaked a few times, all in an attempt to finally put an end to the influence of money on elections and thwart corruption." Adam shifted in his seat and focused on the action on the field as Drew, still chewing his hot dog, kept his eyes on Josh. "As part of that effort," Josh went on, "the Federal Elections Commission was created and they oversaw the regulations put in place including limits on contributions that can made to political candidates." Josh paused as the Rockies center fielder hit a ground ball that managed to roll between the diving Mets shortstop and third baseman.

"Ah, yes," Adam said, whimsically, "you got to love the proverbial ground ball with eyes."

"So those limits on campaign contributions did not apply to contributions to political parties, non-profits, corporations, and unions or affect the advertising those groups did prior to elections, so more recently, the Bipartisan Campaign Reform Act was passed."

"McCain-Feingold," Adam interjected.

"Yeah, yeah," Josh said, fervidly. "So that law was passed in an attempt to restrict the activities and influence of such groups. However, in multiple suits filed to challenge the law, the courts ruled that regulations implemented under the new law were a violation of free speech rights under the First Amendment to the Constitution."

"Wait a minute," Adam blurted out sarcastically, "are you saying the Constitution can be amended?"

Drew rolled his eyes and gave another backhanded smack to Adam's chest as Adam giggled. "Let him finish," Drew said.

"So a foundation called Citizens United led an effort to overturn the regulations in McCain-Feingold, and after the court rulings, special interest groups were subsequently allowed to advertise for election campaigns as long as they did not coordinate activities with a candidate. In another ruling, for SpeechNow.org, other aspects of McCain-Feingold were repudiated that subsequently allowed those groups to raise unlimited funds from individuals, corporations, and unions."

"But the contributions made directly to candidates are still limited, right?" Drew asked.

"Yes" Josh replied. He hesitated as he observed a group of loud fans in the left field bleachers trying to start a stadium wave. "Okay," he continued, "but much of the fund-raising is actually coordinated through political action committees. Different types of political action committees can be established that allow more flexibility in fundraising and spending, but of particular interest are the so-called Super PACs, and with the court rulings, extremely wealthy individuals can donate millions and millions of dollars to a Super PAC and the funds can be used for advertisements on varying issues with specific references to candidates as long as they don't coordinate the activities with any particular candidate."

"Don't forget the 501(c)(4) organizations," Adam chimed in.

"So those non-profit organizations, established based on the stipulations in section 501(c)(4) of the Internal Revenue Code, are allowed to raise money and spend funds on advertising in the same manner, but unlike Super PACs, 501(c)(4) organizations do not have to disclose their donor information."

"And joint fundraising committees?" Adam asked.

"Joint fundraising committees," Drew blurted out. "Is that what you bleeding heart liberals use to raise money to buy joints?"

"So," Josh said, looking at Adam, "joint fundraising committees are formed in the interest of two or more candidates or committees where donors can make large donations that exceed the limits for an individual candidate or committee. Individual candidates or committees are still restricted to only receive money based on individual limits, but multiple candidates or committees can then share the costs, expenses, and efforts associated with fundraising. Donors can make huge donations which has resulted in these committees being called super joint fundraising committees."

"Super joints?" Drew yelled with a booming voice. "You hippies!"

"Are you implying that Republicans aren't using them?" Adam asked Drew.

"What? Joints? Heck no, that nonsense is only for you stoner liberals." Drew turned to face the field as he mumbled, "Frying your brains with that stuff."

"I assure you," Adam said, "Republicans are using joint fundraising committees too."

"Alright," Drew said, turning toward Josh, "I remember all this now." Drew clapped his hands playfully. "Here's what we need, we need a Constitutional convention." The older couple seated three rows in front of them turned to stare at Drew again. Drew gritted his teeth as he looked over at Adam.

"Sorry," Adam said toward the couple. "We can't take this guy anywhere." The couple shook their heads as they turned back around.

"I think he's right," Josh said with a hushed tone. "With the court rulings, there's a new reality now unless a constitutional amendment is passed specifically related to campaign finance reform." They suddenly looked toward the infield as the Rockies pitcher laid down a perfect bunt down the third base line, but the Mets third baseman scurried forward, grabbed the ball with his bare hand, and slung a rope over to first to barely beat the runner racing to the bag. The Rockies center fielder was able to move safely over to second. "It's highly unlikely," Josh went on, "that two-thirds of the House and two-thirds of the Senate would pass such a constitutional amendment, but under Article V of the Constitution, the Constitution can be amended if two-thirds of the states pass a resolution to call for a Constitutional convention and proposed amendments are passed by a two-thirds vote at the convention and the amendments are subsequently ratified by three-fourths of the states."

Drew let out a loud moan as he dropped his head. "Fat chance," Adam mumbled. "Keep in mind that such a Constitutional convention has never happened in the history of America, so even if the states voted for such a convention, it's difficult to predict what would occur."

Drew perked up and said, "They could also pass a balanced budget amendment to the Constitution."

"Oh, come on," Adam groaned. "Drew, we've talked about this. It isn't that simple." Adam paused as they watched the Rockies hitter take a vicious swing and launch a towering shot toward right field but the ball sliced to the right of the foul pole. "Also, consider this," Adam said, "do you think the state legislators aren't mercenaries too? Are you suggesting that they wouldn't be influenced by soft money and wouldn't also pander to big donors and ultimately sabotage any effort toward implementing campaign finance reform? And, all the Senators and Representatives in Washington wouldn't want to lose their power, so they would likely act in some manner before an Article V convention would ever take place, simply to assure they maintain power." Adam paused as they watched another foul ball soar into the upper deck above first base. "Or," Adam said, perking up, forcing a fake smile, "Congress could work up a bipartisan grand plan and fix everything. They could prove, to all the electorate, that despite the billions of dollars spent on elections by special interests, they are indeed there to serve the best interests of the voters that elected them."

Adam, Josh, and Drew became startled as an usher walked down the aisle and began moving along the row in front of them. "Gentlemen," the older usher said, "could you please do me a favor and focus on the game here? I've received three separate complaints in the last five minutes about your gabbing."

"Uh, yes sir," Adam said, his voice breaking. The usher slowly walked away, and Drew scoffed and waved his hand. "Can't talk politics anywhere," Adam whispered.

A resounding crack suddenly echoed in the stadium and the crowd erupted into a roar as the Rockies hitter had tattooed another towering shot that quickly made its way into the right field stands. The stadium's signature homerun music was cued up and animated graphics were displayed on the jumbotron. As the fans cheered, Adam, Josh, and Drew stood up and clapped as they watched the runner finish his trot around the bases.

"It is fascinating," Josh said, leaning toward Adam and Drew to be heard, "you can always tell by the sound off the bat."

With the Rockies now down six to four, Adam commented, "Maybe they can do this." His voice was barely audible over the crowd. "Maybe they can win one for us, while we're here."

Drew playfully raised his knee up and down and smacked his leg to the music. "It's a hoedown," he sang.

The cheering gradually dissipated and they slowly sat down. "I'll say this last thing," Adam said. Josh and Drew leaned in so Adam could whisper. "It really is time. If Congress doesn't want to lose control and watch Constitutional amendments get passed through Article V conventions, they need to act, now. They're facing a three-two count themselves. They've been stalling, fouling off pitches, but the payoff pitch is coming. It's now time for them to, collectively, absolutely tattoo one into the gap and clear the bases. Pass a bipartisan grand plan, now!"

Drew turned toward the field as Josh mumbled, "Don't hold your breath for that. I would guess you're going to see them strikeout."

"Or," Drew said, "if the American public would come to their senses and elect Republicans, Congress could pass the balanced budget amendment we need."

"Or," Josh said, "if the American public would come to their senses and elect Democrats, Congress could pass the campaign finance reform amendment we need."

"What would it take?" Drew asked, glowering at Josh. "What would it take to get you to vote Republican?"

"Explain the math to me."

"What math?"

"You want a balanced budget amendment. From year to year, it's not that simple. But even before considering that, show me the math. Explain to me how you can cut taxes for corporations and the wealthy while maintaining the subsidies for big agribusinesses and big oil companies and protect social security and Medicare, increase defense spending, increase spending for NASA and other

Republican pet projects, and pay the interest on the debt. Show me the math."

"Simple," Drew replied, "you cut welfare, food stamps, and the disability portion of Social Security. And eliminate the EPA and the Department of Education."

"You're so deluded," Josh said. "Show me the math!"

Drew reached around Adam and grabbed Josh's shirt. "Why don't you do some math with this?" he grunted as he jerked on Josh's shirt.

"Alright, alright," Adam yelled, "that's enough. Have you ever realized how I always make a specific point to sit between you two?" Drew released his grip on Josh's shirt but kept staring at him. Josh was stoic as he gazed out at the Mets outfielders. "Indulge me for a minute," Adam said. Adam shook his head and after a couple seconds, he said, "You know what else?"

Drew looked at Adam, and with a sarcastic smile, he said, "What, Adam?"

"The same goes for Kelsey." Drew's smirk receded. "I'll tell you," Adam continued, "Hannah is a hero for caring, but she's right. Kelsey's been heading down a bad path, making so many poor decisions followed by worse decisions. She's facing a three-two count herself. You can see it in her eyes, the malaise, when she's sober. She's not happy at all with where she's ended up. It's like we're peacefully watching her on this insidious, slow-moving descent that is on the cusp of being a full-on train wreck, and if she doesn't respond to this last opportunity, her own payoff pitch, and dispense with those boys right now, change her perspective, and change the way she's living every day, starting right now, well you can forget it. She's a goner." Drew sighed and turned toward the game. Josh slouched in his seat. "It's time for her to swing away and drive one in the gap herself, make some big-time permanent changes."

"Starting this weekend?" Drew questioned.

"Yep."

Chapter 9 – Finances Devalued at the Stadium

Chapter 10 – Rift Felt on Riley Ridge

The bike ride up to Riley Ridge starts at an elevation of 8600 feet, on an old logging road, about a mile down the valley from the ski resort. The climb is gradual in a southerly direction for the first four miles, the double track winding along Riley Creek before the road crosses the creek and becomes much steeper for the ascent up the ridge. Shortly after the stream crossing, the road continues up the east-facing slope with a series of switchbacks and then abruptly changes into a single track above tree line. The path peaks on the rocky ridge at an elevation of 12,100 feet before continuing down into the Wallace Gulch basin.

It was an overcast day that Saturday, but given their early start, they fully expected to be back below tree line before any real threat of inclement weather. The forest around the creek had been thinned several years ago to clear lodgepole pines devastated by pine beetles, but an abundance of aspen, particularly at the bottom of the valley, provided good cover for the diverse wildlife that inhabited the area along the gulch.

Adam, Hannah, Josh, Emily, Justin, and Kelsey all rode together at the beginning as Kelsey, Emily, and Hannah gossiped, either about Emily's coworkers at the resort lodge or workers on Kelsey's landscaping crews. Kelsey was pedaling a cheaper rigid bike she borrowed from Hannah's friend as Hannah and Emily rode their matching full suspension bikes. Hannah and Emily bought their mountain bikes at the same time during their second summer in Spruce Creek and this ride was another in a long series of rides they enjoyed together. Adam rode his new full suspension bike with twenty-nine inch wheels as Josh cranked toe clips on the pedals of his older hardtail bike with twenty-six inch wheels.

Adam and Josh listened to the girls' gossip and couldn't help but get caught up in the discussion as they often see the subjects at popular events around the valley. Justin was riding his cheap rigid bike that had a worn chain that rattled as it passed through the derailleur and over the gears on the rear cassette. Justin's breathing was labored, so Josh set an easier pace to allow them to stay together for a while. Cody was also on the adventure and certainly wouldn't have any trouble keeping up, but Hannah wanted to maintain a slower pace at first to not wear out their nine-year-old best friend.

Flows in Riley Creek were low as the snowmelt runoff was long over. Several beaver dams along the creek created large ponds with the water backing up on the road in a few spots. Numerous mature aspen had been gnawed, and the downed trees were used by beavers to build impressive dams, the largest of which was one hundred feet across and four feet high and afforded one of the better fishing holes in the valley. One-inch diameter, polyvinyl chloride pipes had been installed by forest service personnel in a few of the structures to assure enough water passes to prevent major damage to the road foundation. The road is still key for workers accessing the forest to complete fuel reduction projects to reduce the risk of forest fires.

When they reached the stream crossing, the flow was so low that each of them was able to, one-by-one, carry out a bumpy roll across the rocky stream bed, and as they initiated the steeper ascent up the ridge, conversations faded and they all settled into their individual pedaling rates. Josh and Adam were of course quickly out in front, initiating yet another one of their signature races to the next stopping point. Nobody else cared to join the competition. Kelsey rode about thirty feet behind them and had begun to sing to herself. Justin promptly drifted back and was barely out of view from Hannah and Emily. They all agreed to stop at a fork, right before the third switchback.

Josh might have beaten Adam to the stopping point, but as they powered toward the finish, Josh came up on a grouse that was bedded in the tall grass between the double tracks. The grouse was initially unnoticeable, but as they approached, the bird took flight, right in front of Josh's front tire, startling him and causing him to stop as the grouse fluttered its wings loudly and elevated past his head. Josh was so flustered by the grouse that Adam was able to seize the opportunity to pedal past him and maintained his lead to the stopping point. Kelsey, Hannah, and Emily strolled up behind them shortly thereafter. They all took a moment to catch their breathes and hydrate. Cody had been running about and rummaging in the forest but soon joined them as they gathered.

A few minutes later, Justin trundled up, gasping for air. "Sorry," he mumbled as he slowly stepped off his bike, leaned down, and rested his right elbow on his bike seat. Kelsey trudged over and put her arm around him, unaffected by his shirt that was drenched in sweat. The rest of them continued with their discussion about the potential deal Josh may have to sell framed pictures for units in the new resort condo building. They were arguing over whether Josh's pictures of the aurora borealis should be included in the potential collection.

Kelsey kept rubbing Justin's shoulders and whispered, "Do you remember that energy you had when you snapped that pool cue in two?" Justin was sheepish as he responded with a slight nod. "I want you to find that energy and channel that energy into those quads for this next section of the ride."

Justin arched an eyebrow as he peered up at Kelsey. "Sure," he grunted.

"I'm serious. Think about that moment as you keep pedaling. Where do you think I'm getting my energy? I'm not in great shape. Find your rage and release all that rage on Riley Ridge."

"Kelsey," Justin whispered, his breathing still ragged, "we need to talk some more about the rage you're harboring–"

"Justin," Hannah called, "explain the aurora borealis to me."

Justin smiled, but before he could start, Kelsey interjected, "No, no, let me try this one. I heard a story about this on NPR the other day."

Emily nudged Hannah and whispered, "I told you."

Kelsey looked back at Justin and said, "The professor can grade me on this." Kelsey let out a deep sigh as she turned toward Hannah but stayed close to Justin, her side pressed up against him. "Okay," she started, "so there's a stream of charged particles emitted from the sun."

"Solar wind," Josh mumbled.

Emily smacked Josh on the chest, causing him to grunt. "Let her finish," she admonished.

"As the particles reach Earth," Kelsey went on, looking down at the ground, "the particles get deflected by the Earth's magnetic field, or they get trapped in the Van Allen radiation belt, but some particles get channeled toward the North Pole and South Pole."

Kelsey paused as she shifted, resting more of her weight against Justin, and Justin, still bent over with his elbow on his bike seat, seemed to become transfixed from his exhaustion, from Kelsey's touch, and from the discussion. As Kelsey gathered her thoughts, Adam took a couple steps to the side and sat on a large rock. Hannah walked over and sat next to him, placing her hand on his knee. Cody scurried over and nudged between them and leaned his head back as Adam gently petted him.

"When there's a strong solar wind," Kelsey continued slowly, "the charged particles that enter the Earth's atmosphere at the poles react with the Nitrogen and Oxygen …atoms and molecules."

"Ionization," Justin whispered. "Photons are emitted."

Kelsey perked up and said, "And then you have a beautiful luminosity around the poles, so in the north, you can see the Northern Lights." Kelsey looked up as she mellifluously finished, "or your Aurora Borealis." Kelsey had a big grin on her face as she looked at Justin. "Good?" she asked.

"Ah, what do I know?"

Kelsey looked at Josh and asked, "What color are the Northern Lights in your pictures?"

"Mostly green, some red," Josh replied. "Alright," he said, clearing his throat and grabbing his bike, "let's move." Adam quickly stood up, somewhat rudely brushing Hannah away. He grabbed his bike and was promptly pedaling up the road with Josh as Cody bolted ahead. The others slowly filed in behind them.

The road was rocky for the remaining two miles up the ridge and more difficult to navigate but still ridable. With a mile remaining, trees in the forest were more sparse. Grasses and weeds around the double tracks were denser. The back side of the ski resort could be seen to the east, including a favorite run of theirs, Gus's Glade. Seven years ago, on one of the most epic powder days in resort history, Adam and Hannah met while skiing in the trees off to the side of Gus's Glade.

When they arrived at the single track, Adam managed to pedal out in front for the final segment up the rutted dirt path to the ridge. Above tree line, they could all see each other, and while everyone was breathing heavily, they were content to keep moving and finish the ascent. Adam reached the top first. Josh had opportunities to pedal off the trail and over the alpine tundra to get around Adam, but he never got it done. He was visibly displeased with himself. Kelsey, Hannah, and Emily arrived shortly thereafter.

While it can be quite windy at the top of the ridge, it was pleasant, at least for the moment. The ridge around the trail was rocky and jagged and barren of any vegetation in the immediate vicinity. The perch offered a three-hundred-and-sixty-degree panoramic view. The Wallace Gulch valley could be seen to the west in front of the high peaks farther off in the distance. With the good monsoon season rains that summer, the Wallace Gulch valley was exceptionally green for being July. A dirt, forest service road could be seen that extended all the way up the Wallace Gulch valley before terminating above tree line at the remnants of an old silver mine located in the southeast corner of the bowl, near the head of the valley. A steady stream of water, originating from two natural springs, fed into Wallace Gulch, and the flow rumbling down the bowl could be heard faintly as the water progressed over the tundra before disappearing into the pines.

Farther down the valley, Porcupine Notch could be seen, at a low point on the west ridge of the Wallace Gulch valley, and the entire stretch of a paved bike path could be viewed that runs from the highway to Porcupine Notch before continuing over to the next valley. Dead trees from the pine beetles had been cleared near the bike path in separate areas leaving three trapezoidal-shaped sections that were completely denuded of trees. The cleared areas were actually quite large, but from that vantage point, the fuels reduction areas seemed tiny relative to the size of the forest. A wisp of smoke could be seen from one slash pile that was burning.

To the north, Mount Preston and Higgins Peak towered over the disc golf course, the highway, and the civilization around Spruce Creek. To the east, a large portion of the Spruce Creek valley could be seen including the Spruce Creek golf course directly below them, the North Fork Tavern, and several ski runs on the hillside to the south.

Josh, looking to the south toward the backside of the ski resort, was suddenly gripped by something in his line of sight. He stepped over and nudged Adam.

"What do you got?" Adam asked as he looked in the same direction.

"Moose and a calf, right under the El Otro Lado lift, about a quarter of the way up."

Adam scanned for several seconds before noting, "Ah, yeah, I see." Emily casually strolled over to assess the situation.

Kelsey, with her head down, sat on a low bedrock outcrop. She pulled her knees up in front of her and began singing softly to herself. Hannah sat beside her. Kelsey turned her head and kept singing softly as she looked into Hannah's green eyes. Emily sat on a larger rock, and Josh managed to sit beside her on a knobby boulder that was certainly not the most ideal place to sit, but he was close to Emily. Adam looked over at Hannah. He stared right at her for several seconds before she finally noticed. He scrunched his nose and stuck his tongue out at her. She responded with the same gesture.

Justin was thoroughly frazzled and his breathing was shaky as he finally completed his final cranks and eased up on his bike. The others didn't look at him or say anything as he dropped his bike and paced around, wheezing. Josh motioned toward Adam and asked, "Hey, did you hear about that latest bombing in Yemen?" Adam groaned and nodded. "Justin," Josh said, "I got one for you, so how would you encapsulate the Sunni versus Shia conflict?"

Justin, drenched in sweat and holding his water bottle, let out a deep sigh before he took another gulp of water. He put his hands on his hips and rested his arms akimbo as he said in a breathy reply, "You already know all about that."

"But help me out," Josh said, "so the overwhelming majority of Muslims in the world are Sunni, right? And Shias, which are a minority in most Muslim countries, are often supported by Iran, one country where the population is largely comprised of Shias." Justin nodded as he was starting to get his breath back. "The differences all began nearly fourteen hundred years ago, right? Over the successor to the prophet Muhammad." Emily groaned, closed her eyes, and leaned her head against Josh's shoulder. "The Shias believe the guidance and the religious authority of the prophet was passed on to Muhammad's descendants, whereas the Sunnis believe in the traditions established under the prophet Muhammad." Justin hemmed and hawed a bit and nodded.

Kelsey stopped singing and began to snivel as she purred, "Hannah." She turned toward Hannah and put her arms around her. Hannah was thrown off by Kelsey's embrace but adjusted herself to get into a comfortable position to hug her back.

"Sunnis and Shias have political, social, and cultural differences today," Josh went on, still looking at Justin for confirmation, "in regards to their core values and their rituals related to marriage, dress, and the role of Islam in determining laws." Josh hesitated and Justin nodded slowly.

Kelsey shifted her legs and nuzzled up closer to Hannah and whined again, "Hannah?"

Hannah whispered, "What is it, sweetie?"

"Here's what I don't understand," Adam chimed in. "Sunnis and Shias agree on so much. Both sects believe the prophet, Muhammad, was the messenger for one God, Allah. The two sects agree on much in regards to the practices of Islam including fasting during Ramadan, an annual pilgrimage to Mecca, and five prayers a day, and they also share the holy book, the Quran."

"Well, descendants of Muhammad were assassinated," Justin said, "which, by the way, partly contributes to the role of martyrdom in Shia culture. Anyway, while sure, that happened centuries ago, there has been so much discrimination and so much resentment over past events that it has led to strong sectarian violence throughout Muslim societies. But yes, you're right, it should be emphasized that notwithstanding the mutual enmity, the two sects have lived peacefully together for long periods of time before and also noted that most Sunnis and Shias live together now, quite peacefully."

Kelsey grabbed Hannah tightly and pulled on her. Kelsey had begun moaning in anguish. "Hannah," Kelsey groaned as she started to rock back and forth.

Hannah's eyes got real big as she looked up at Adam and then over at Emily, but she couldn't make eye contact with either of them. Hannah looked back at Kelsey and asked, "What is it?"

Kelsey, with her face buried against Hannah, bellowed, "Make them stop."

"Some of the recent strife could be traced back to territorial borders," Adam continued.

Kelsey screeched, "Hannah," drawing the attention of Emily.

"Adam," Hannah called.

"Borders drawn after World War I," Adam went on, looking at Josh, "do not match the geographical distribution of the two sects."

"Adam," Hannah yelled, stridently. Adam, startled, looked at her.

"What?"

"Stop it."

Kelsey was now wailing. She clenched tightly to Hannah. Hannah's eyes were open wide as she looked at Emily and then back at Adam. Hannah shrugged her shoulders and silently mouthed, "I don't know."

Kelsey, now with a vice grip on Hannah, bawled for several seconds. Cody had been roaming around nearby but responded to Kelsey cries. He lumbered up to her and stuck his nose under her arm. "Cody, no," Hannah commanded. "Get him," she said to Adam. Adam snapped his fingers once and Cody promptly lumbered over. They all remained quiet and were on tenterhooks as they kept looking at each other, struggling to assess the reason for Kelsey's breakdown. After a minute, Kelsey relaxed but was still sobbing lightly.

"Kelsey," Adam said, "we're sorry. We're so sorry."

"Good for you," Emily yelled. "Somebody needed to finally shut these guys up." Josh, with a stern look on his face, glared back at Emily.

Kelsey whispered into Hannah's ear, where the others couldn't hear, "Can I talk to Justin?"

"Sure. Justin, she wants to talk to you. Come here." Hannah slowly pulled Kelsey's grip away. As she stood up, she held both of Kelsey's wrists. Justin slowly walked over. "Sit right there," Hannah said. As Justin sat, Kelsey latched on to him in the same manner she had been holding Hannah. Justin was clearly uncomfortable, but he put his arms around her, awkwardly.

"Hey," Josh said to Justin, "we're going to roll back down the trail a bit toward that overlook where we can get a better view of the front side of the resort. I want to take some pictures of the ski hill from there. We'll eat our snacks there."

"Take your time," Hannah said to Justin. "We'll wait there."

Cody nuzzled back up to Kelsey's side as Adam, Hannah, Josh, and Emily picked up their bikes and coasted down the path. As they drifted out of sight, Adam called for Cody and he instantly took off down the trail.

Justin was still as he held Kelsey for several seconds before he softly asked, "What's up?"

"My brother," Kelsey whimpered.

"You have a brother?"

"I had a brother."

Justin suddenly became loose and slouched as if losing control of his body weight. "Oh Kelsey. Kelsey, I'm so sorry. I didn't know. What happened?"

"He was killed in Iraq!"

"Oh," Justin groaned. "Oh, Kelsey." He pulled her into him. She pulled back to shift one of her legs behind him and straddled his side, latching back onto him. "Kelsey, Kelsey, Kelsey." He kissed her forehead. "Kelsey, I'm so sorry. When?"

"My sophomore year in high school," she mumbled with a sniffle.

"Does Hannah know?"

"No, and I don't want to tell them."

"Okay. That's fine. Why?"

"I'm sick of all the pity, Justin."

"Okay, hey," Justin said, pulling back and waiting for her to look up. She slowly lifted her head. Her cheeks were red and her eyes were bloodshot. "I will never tell anyone, okay?" Kelsey dropped her head back down and rested it against his chest.

"Gosh, your parents too. Oh Kelsey, no wonder. I can't even imagine what they went through, how they changed, how it altogether changed the way they treated you. They probably wanted to lock you up and protect you from everything." Justin grabbed Kelsey tightly. "Kelsey, Kelsey, Kelsey."

Justin held her close and calmly for a couple minutes as he periodically kissed her forehead and stroked her head. She gradually became relaxed and wiped her eyes a few times but continued to hold him.

"You know what?" he said. "You're right. Pity doesn't help. What you need right now is for everyone to treat you normally, with admiration and respect. That's what you deserve. Gosh, if anyone came up to you and began talking to you like you were some helpless five year old, I would want to break them in two. That's something else you probably look to escape from. I guess that's probably one thing you can count on from those dang boys. As insensitive and crass as they can be, they probably never express any pity. Meanwhile, everyone else is so sure they have such brilliant advice to render."

Justin sighed a couple times as he held Kelsey. He gazed off in the distance toward two ATVs and a dirt motor bike that were driving up the forest service road in Wallace Gulch. As the tiny specks were getting close to the silver mine remains, the sound of the revving dirt bike engine could be heard echoing off the valley walls. Justin, now seeming perfectly comfortable in his embrace with Kelsey, then became distracted by a Rocky Mountain marmot that poked up out of the rocks about sixty feet in front of him. The marmot, a little over a foot long with brown fur, a yellow belly, and a rounded snout, sat and stared back at Justin. Justin loosened his grip on Kelsey, causing her to soften her grip, but they remained still. As Justin stared at the marmot, the marmot began periodically letting off loud, sharp whistles which got Kelsey's attention. She twisted her head, and at that moment, another marmot poked up out of the rocks. Kelsey caressed Justin's back as they both watched the two marmots for a minute. The marmots continued with their signature whistles every few seconds. Kelsey sloughed more of her weight against Justin. She slowly turned her head up and kissed him on the chin, and with her second kiss, thunder rumbled off to the west.

"Hey," Justin said, "I do want to hold you all day, but we should probably start heading down. Are you ready?"

Kelsey nodded and released her grasp. She got up and wiped her nose real good with the side of her hand. They grabbed their bikes and coasted down the rutted path. As they reached the spot where Adam, Hannah, Josh, and Emily had stopped, Kyle was there, standing over his custom-made full suspension bike and talking to Josh about the conditions on the trail. Justin clumsily skidded sideways as he approached and almost laid his bike down, barely avoiding Kyle. Kyle's manner turned dour as he glared at Justin. Kelsey, with her eyes still watery and her cheeks red, eased up behind Justin. Hannah promptly stepped over and hugged Kelsey gently and awkwardly as Kelsey stood over her bike.

"I'm going to coast on down," Justin said. "I'm a wimp on the downhill, so I'm sure you'll catch me before the stream crossing."

"Okay," Adam replied. Adam looked at Kelsey. "Kelsey," he said, calmly, "again, I'm so sorry." Kelsey responded with an offhanded nod. "There's an intent with this entire discussion. I promise. I'll impart that to you another day, but there is a reason why Josh and I keep getting caught up on these topics."

"Whatever," Kelsey mumbled. She peered down the trail at Justin. "I'm going to head down too," she keenly said.

"Okay," Hannah said. Kelsey rolled away. "We're right behind you," Hannah said loudly.

Hannah looked at Adam and raised her eyebrows. Emily smacked her hand against her forehead, and Josh smiled before slowly saying, "The Phlox and the Wallflower."

"Oh boy," Emily said. "Guys, what have you done?"

Chapter 11 – Wiggles Witnesses Crisis

Adam lay peacefully on his stomach with blankets wrapped snuggly around his shoulders. Hannah turned on the overhead lights in the bedroom, but Adam, already in a deep sleep for over two hours, was unaffected by her movements that Saturday night.

"Adam," Hannah softly called as she stood at the end of the bed. There was no response. Adam's breathing was steady and calm. Hannah, still wearing her light blue, plaid, cotton sleeping shorts and a yellow, three-quarter sleeved pajama top, switched on the lamp at Adam's side of the bed. There was still no response. Hannah sighed as she looked over at Cody who was also sound asleep on the end of the bed. Hannah gently sat on the bed, crossed her legs, and rested her hand on Adam's back. She felt his torso rise ever so gently with each inhale. As she pulled her hand back, she let out another deep sigh which awoke Cody, but he remained motionless. Cody's eyes were now open and he watched Hannah slouch and rest her chin on her hand.

"Adam," Hannah called again at a normal volume.

Adam groaned lightly. He noticed the light from the lamp, twitched, and jerked his head away. "Adam, I'm sorry, we need to go check on Kelsey."

"No," he grumbled, his voice muffled. "I told you we weren't doing that again."

"Adam, we have to. It's our fault. I don't know why she broke down today, but she's a mess."

Adam groaned as he twisted over to his back and covered his eyes with his hand.

"Adam," Hannah pouted.

"Call Justin."

"Adam."

"I'm serious."

"I can't call Justin. You call him." Adam pulled his arm from under the covers and stretched it out, holding out his hand. Hannah jumped up abruptly, startling Cody and causing him to raise his head. She grabbed Adam's phone off the dresser, found Justin's number in his contacts, and made the call. Adam had one eye open as he took the phone. He peered back at Hannah, scrunched his nose, and stuck his tongue out at her. After several rings, Justin answered.

"What's up, boss?" Adam asked whimsically. Hannah could hear Justin's voice but couldn't make out what he was saying. "I don't even know," Adam said. Adam turned his head and asked Hannah, "What time is it?"

"1:30."

Adam groaned and mumbled, "Dude, I'm sorry, but could you please go check on Kelsey? We'll make it up to you somehow. I don't know how, but we'll do something. I promise." Hannah leaned in and tried to decipher Justin's response. "I don't know, man. Same deal, I guess." Cody let out a soft whimper as he dropped his head down on the bed. "Yeah," Adam said, "just go talk to her. We had a setback today, but I seriously think we're making progress."

Adam looked at Hannah and shook his head over Justin's negative response. Hannah leaned toward the phone and cried, "Justin, please."

Adam listened for a few seconds before saying, "I tell you what, I'll read your paper."

"I'll read it too," Hannah blurted out loudly.

"I'm serious. We will both read your journal article tomorrow morning. We already have the link. Justin, I promise you, we will both read it." Adam looked up at Hannah and smiled. "Yeah, walk around the back. Her sliding glass door will probably be open." Adam chuckled as he listened to Justin's response. "I don't know," Adam added. "I guess she likes to encourage intruders. Anybody who tried to walk in on her would get their ass beaten anyway." Adam rolled to his side. "Yes, we'll read it. Justin, I promise. We'll talk to you about it the next time we see you at the North Fork, okay?"

Hannah leaned toward the phone and yelled, "Thank you, Justin."

Adam ended the call, handed his phone to Hannah, and mumbled, "We're good."

"What's his paper about?"

"Cloud seeding," Adam said, smiling. "Oh my goodness Hannah, he was so excited when I told him we would read his paper. I bet we could have gotten him to drive to Denver if that was involved. But we're on the hook now. Seriously, we have to read his paper tomorrow."

"Okay," Hannah said. She fervently hopped up, set Adam's phone on the dresser, and turned out the lights. She slowly slid into bed and nuzzled up to Adam. "I love you so much," she whispered. Adam, lying on his back, had already closed his eyes and let out a soft moan. "No, no, no," she said sweetly, climbing on top of him, "you're not going back to sleep now."

When Justin arrived at Kelsey's place, the sliding glass door was not only unlocked but was wide open. It was cold inside, though the living room still reeked of cigarette smoke. Justin, wearing a solid pullover and blue jeans, entered and slammed the door behind him. "Kelsey," he yelled, "you're going to keep this door closed and locked from now on." He flipped the switch to turn on the gas fireplace. He took a couple steps toward the middle of the room, and put his hands on his hips. With his arms akimbo, he looked around the living room, the dining room, and the kitchen. "I thought Adam cleaned this place up," he mumbled to himself.

Kelsey's roommate's cat, Wiggles, sauntered around the corner from the hallway.

"Justin?" Kelsey called from her bedroom, clearly excited to hear his baritone voice.

"Yeah."

Shaking his head, Justin commenced picking up pieces of junk mail and started a pile for dirty clothes. Wiggles jumped up on the old, wooden dining room table and then up on the bar between the kitchen and dining room. She sat, peacefully, and watched Justin pick up clothes and trash.

Suddenly, Kelsey, wearing an over-sized t-shirt and shorts, came rumbling out of her bedroom. Her hair was tousled and her makeup was smudged. She stumbled into the door jam and then into the hallway wall. Then, with her head down, she initiated a sprint and ran full speed at Justin. She lunged at him, ramming her shoulder into his gut, lifting his weight off the floor before slamming him into the sofa. He instinctively fought back, and while he tried to get out from under her, before he knew it, she was straddling him and pulling at his shirt.

"Kelsey, stop it!"

"She froze for a couple seconds. Then, she began to laugh as she pulled again on his shirt."

"Kelsey, I'm serious. Stop it." Kelsey paused again, her mouth agape. He managed to wrestle his legs out from under her as she sat mystified, in awe over his refusal. "Kelsey, you're such a tart. Why are you like this?" Kelsey pulled her head back and instantly became inflamed. She gritted her teeth and with scorn, pulled her right arm back, and slapped him hard across the cheek.

"What the hell?" Justin exclaimed as he put his hand on his face.

Kelsey shoved him as she got up and marched back to her bedroom.

"Damn," Justin grunted. "Kelsey, I'm sorry. Come here." He shifted on the sofa and set his feet on the floor. Wiggles was wholly focused on the quarrel and became uneasy but remained seated on the bar. Justin slowly leaned down. With his elbows on his knees, he rested his head in his hands. Kelsey, with her clothes all mussed and her face puce with rage, came storming out of her room again, and with fury, she ran at him and thrusted him down on the couch. She began walloping him repeatedly, smacking him in the head twice. After taking several strikes to the arms, Justin finally managed to grab both her wrists, and with no hesitation, she charged at his left shoulder with her teeth. Wiggles stood up on the bar and began wailing. Her caterwauling didn't deter Kelsey. Kelsey lunged to chomp on Justin's trapezius muscle, but she wasn't able to get a good bite. Justin finally mustered up a surge of strength and managed to push her back on the sofa. He used his knees to pin both her legs. He held her wrists over her head. Kelsey hissed as she squirmed aggressively to get loose, but she eventually became exhausted.

"Kelsey," Justin said. She let out a roar in response, causing Wiggles to unleash another shriek. "Kelsey, listen to me." Kelsey kept wiggling her legs in an attempt to get free. "Kelsey, I'm love with somebody else."

Kelsey froze. Her rage was still simmering, but she had become completely frozen as she furrowed her brow and stared back into Justin's eyes. Her muscles very slowly began to relax. A smile eventually overtook her face, and she burst out laughing. Her entire body went limp. She lay back, prostrate, as she twisted her head back and forth, cackling. Justin let go of her wrists and sat up on the sofa. He narrowed his eyes and stuck out his lower lip as he watched her laugh and laugh and laugh.

After several seconds, Kelsey regained her composure. "Who is she?" she asked. Justin shook his head. He shoved her legs off the sofa. Kelsey pulled herself up. "Okay, I'm sorry," she said, still chuckling. "Justin, I'm sorry. Who is she?"

"You don't know her." Kelsey shifted closer to him, pressing up against him. "Justin, we have to tell her."

"No," he cried. "It doesn't matter. Look, she's gone."

"Where?"

"Kelsey, she's just out there. It wasn't going to happen. There was never any chance of anything happening." Kelsey slouched back against the sofa. Wiggles lost interest in the situation and turned her head away. "Kelsey, look, consider all those times when some guy was all head-over-heels for you, and you knew, but you never gave it any thought. I know you know exactly what I'm talking about, where you didn't lose a wink of sleep over it or dwell on it for a single second. As soon as you figured it out, you concluded that the fella was simply going to have to get over it and move on, right?"

"Justin, this is …so …stupid." Kelsey reached her hand over and rubbed his chest. "So that's it? You're done?" she asked. "All this time that you've been sulking around and hiding in your own little world, you were pining for this lost love." Justin dropped his head. Kelsey evinced her exhaustion from their scuffle and slowly lay back on the sofa. She grabbed a throw pillow off the floor and placed it behind her head. "She wedged her feet between Justin and the sofa as she tried to reach up and grab his hand. "Justin, come here."

"Kelsey."

"No, I know. Lie with me. Justin, please, this is for me. Please, for me, lie down with me here."

After a few seconds, Justin slowly let himself gently fall over her. He sloughed his weight off to her side. His face was resting against her belly. Kelsey reached both her hands down over him and rubbed his back. In about three slow movements, he slowly eased his head up to her shoulder and nuzzle his face against her neck. She gently ran her hand through the curls in his hair and managed to deftly slide one of her legs under him so he was lying between her legs. Continuing to run her fingers through his brown locks, she reached out with her other arm and grabbed a blanket off the floor and threw it over them.

"Kelsey, I'm sorry," he said with a whimper. "You're not a tart. I don't know why I said that. After these last few days, I now know more than ever, more than anybody maybe, what an amazing, incredible person you are." Kelsey shushed him as she pulled her knees up and gently put both her arms down over his back.

"Tell me about her," she whispered.

"Oh Kelsey, she's so beautiful. But that's not why I fell in love with her. She's so bright and so fun. Kelsey, that smile. She's so loving to anyone. She is such a dream to be around for anyone, kids, old people."

"What happened?"

"Nothing happened," he mumbled, as he pressed his face against her neck.

"How long did you go out?"

"We didn't"

Kelsey shifted her head off to the side in an effort to look into his eyes. "Justin, what the hell?" she yelled. He sighed deeply as she asked, "She wasn't your girlfriend?" Justin shook his head gently as he kept his face buried against her neck. "And you never told her?" Justin nuzzled further into her. "Justin, I'm sorry, but this is ...so ...stupid."

"Kelsey, that's not fair."

Kelsey pulled him into her and patted his back as she shook her head. "Here's the thing," she started, "when people become so infatuated, it starts when they attach all these perfect qualities that aren't even close to being real. A person becomes obsessed with this idea of somebody, somebody who doesn't exist. Sure, she may be gorgeous and attractive, but are you sure you didn't create a person in your mind and create a vision in regards to the role that this person might play in your life along with so much else about their personality and character, that wasn't even real?" Justin remained still. "Justin, you may be hung up on a person that is a ridiculous fantasy, that doesn't even exist. Look, your right, boys have been infatuated with me, but it soon becomes clear that I'm not even the person they're obsessed with. Come on, I'm a frickin' train wreck. They couldn't handle me for one week." Kelsey sighed and shook her head as she looked off to the side. She gently ran her fingers through his hair. "Gosh," she mumbled, "I wonder how many people in this world are all alone because of love. It is ironic, isn't it?"

"Well," Justin responded, his voice muffled as he talked into her neck, "how many people are together who don't love each other? How many people get together because everything seemed so perfect on paper, but they never felt anything for each other?"

"Wow, so it's one and done for you?" Kelsey asked. She sighed and spoke on softly, "Justin, this is …so …stupid. You have to stop pining for this girl. We've all be jilted. Everyone's been jilted. You move on. Heck, you told me to move on a few days ago."

Justin wiggled his entire body as he tried to nuzzle closer to her. Kelsey reached both her hands down over his back and pulled him against her as she gently kissed his earlobe. She slowly encircled her legs around him and pulled him in closer. He responded with timid caresses to her arm, and suddenly, sure, inspired, he pushed firmly against her. He grabbed her shoulders and pressed his mouth against hers but quickly pulled back.

"It's okay," she whispered. "Justin, you've helped me so much these past few days, I want to help you." His breathing became ragged, the pleasure of her contact took control as she caressed his back and kissed his eyebrows. She slowly began to move her hips, and he responded, pressing hard against her again and holding there. "Trust me," she whispered, "everything will be fine."

Justin gave in, set free of the inhibitions that had controlled him for so long. Following her call, his lips touched her cheek. Her lips quickly found his. Her sudden warmth invigorated him, and weak with desire and having reached a breaking point, they frantically disrobed. Their bodies were now touching all over and undulating together. He became even more drawn to her, he felt her become powerless, and he rose up. She was docile as she looked up at him and watched him, suspended over her. Her eagerness evinced by beads of sweat quivering on her lips while she waited. Then, she giggled with delight over his readiness. He slowly whispered, "I have no idea what I'm doing," but then asserted his will over her.

As he continued to explore her, all of her, he embraced the vibration running through him. Kelsey suddenly opened her eyes as he heard him sniffle gently. She turned her head and saw his eyes well up. She gritted her teeth and smacked him hard with the sides of her fists. "Don't you dare do that," she admonished. He buried his face against her neck and soon felt her become powerless again. As the breeze of his movements flowed through her nerves, she clung to him even tighter.

Nearer to his discovery of her, a fire also flew over her. Her chest heaved against him, and they breathed heavily together before crying together in agony, ecstasy. Then, quiet, only their breathing could be heard as he sank over her. Justin, breathing heavily, lay with most of his weight over her, his head over her shoulder and his face buried in the sofa pillow. She patted him on the back several times and ran her other hand through his hair as he slowly began to get his breath back. He slowly slid off to the side and rose up off the sofa.

Kelsey lay alone as she waited. With her hand over her forehead and her eyes wide open, she stared at the ceiling. "What the hell," she mouthed to herself. After a minute, Justin returned. He nimbly lay to her side, sinking his body between her and the back of the sofa. He managed to reach the blanket on the floor and adroitly covered both of them before resting his head against her shoulder. Wiggles let out a sigh of a purr. She hopped off the kitchen counter to the kitchen table and jumped down to the floor before slinking off to the bedroom.

"Justin," Kelsey said, "who's Whitney?"

Justin's breath hitched. He squeezed his eyes shut and gritted his teeth for a couple seconds. "Uh," he droned before opening his eyes and staring blankly across the room.

"Is that her?" Justin squeezed his eyes shut again and grimaced. "Really?" Kelsey yelled. "You're locked in the clench with me and you say her name?"

"Damn," Justin whispered to himself. He raised his head up. His teeth were still clenched.

"Are you kidding me?" Kelsey asked again as she began hitting him with the side of her fist.

"I'm sorry," he said, ducking his head away from her strikes. He reached up with his arm and managed to catch her wrist and pull it down against her belly. He let out a deep sigh as he buried his face against her shoulder.

"Justin, this is …so …stupid. Please tell me you know that. You do know that, right? Look, I don't care that you said another girl's name. That doesn't make me mad. I'm mad that you're being such an idiot about this." Kelsey turned her head and talked softly into his ear. "Look, you have so much love to give. You have so much need for love." Justin released her arm and then pushed his hand under her to hold her.

"Kelsey, I'm sorry."

"Well," she said, looking up at the ceiling, "I will tell you this, Whitney missed out. I'm the lucky beneficiary of all that pinned up affection and energy. How long have you been holding that in for her?" Justin rose and shook his head slowly. "Hey, listen to me," she said, "you remember, when we were hiking up to Mount Preston and you compared me to that endangered wildflower, the Phlox something?" Justin nodded. "There are endangered types of wallflowers too, right?" Justin didn't respond.

They lay in silence for a couple minutes, gently caressing each other. Justin eventually rose up on his elbow and pulled the blanket off her. In the dim light, he looked at her. He looked her up and down. Kelsey was unaffected as he examined her. She relaxed her head back, put her hand to her forehead again, and shook her head gently as she stared up at the ceiling.

"Kelsey, how about you? I worry that you see yourself as this helpless girl, but please hear me, you are not a train wreck. I've said this before. You are a beautiful, strong, empowered woman. What you felt from me was not some pinned up fire that I had for another girl and it wasn't solely due to the powerful allure you have. What happened there was about the person I got to know this past week. The person that you are, on the inside." Kelsey, with her body still fully exposed for his examination, reached up and ran her fingers through his hair. "Kelsey, do you know that 1980s song, Dreaming, by Blondie, Debbie Harry? I want you to listen to the lyrics of that song and sing them. I'm telling you, what you need has been right in front of you."

Kelsey began to sing softly, "I sit by and watch the river flow." She slowly slid her left leg under him and locked him between her legs again. "I sit by and watch the traffic go," she crooned, caressing his back.

"Kelsey, you're not letting me finish my thought. I'm trying to tell you something."

"Imagine something of your very own," she continued singing as her eyes glistened.

She pulled him down over her. He didn't resist. Her determination was clear, and he yielded. She would have her satisfaction again, seizing her privilege again. Holding him against her, and she nearer to him, her touch was even more bracing and sent a thrill over him, rendering him speechless. He was instantly panting and teeming with desire yet again. He ducked his head and began to enjoy her anew. "Something you can have and hold," she sang with a mellifluous hum. Lost in himself again, driven again, he kissed her gently on the lips before she could sing another word. Feeling his movement against her, she pressed her lips to his, and he pressed against her. After he felt a flame flow through her again, he rose up. She glowed intimately as she waited for him and then accepted him again. They clung to each other, tightly, as he attended to her even more skillfully than the first time and felt the tremors take hold of her.

Wiggles sat peacefully in the hallway as she watched their renewed adventure. She eventually let out another sigh of a purr and slinked back to the bedroom. Kelsey lay, waiting, breathing steadily and staring at the ceiling when Justin returned. He lay beside her as she sang softly, "I'd build a road in gold, just to have some dreaming."

"Kelsey, I need to tell you something."

"Let's go sit outside."

"Kelsey, it's nearly 3:00 a.m."

"Oh, it's still the shank of the evening, come on."

"It's freezing."

"No, we can both squeeze in my sleeping bag and lie on the chair out there."

"Kelsey, I need to tell you something."

Kelsey wiggled out from under his leg and got up. Justin sighed as he sat up, but he soon became transfixed as he leered at her naked body walking away. He scanned her thoroughly as she scurried over to the coat closet and pulled out a sleeping bag. The bag was stuffed in its carrying sack and she swiftly pulled at end of the bag and furiously jerked to get the sleeping bag out of its sack. "Come on," she said, "this thing's rated to like forty below." She plodded briskly over to the sliding glass door and yanked on the door. The door, now locked, rattled loudly in the jam. "Who the hell locked this door?" she chided as a scowl briefly fell over her face. With a grunt, she flipped the lock and stepped outside.

Quickly stepping into the bag, she zipped it up halfway, and sat on an old reclining chair. "Get that cute butt out here," she called. Justin frenetically threw the blanket off him, turned out the lights, and scurried out to the patio. After quietly closing the sliding glass door behind him, he slipped his legs into the sleeping bag, and they both struggled, for a couple minutes, to get comfortable. But after some fairly intense but quiet bickering, they managed to get the bag zipped up with both of them inside. There was no room for either of them to move, and both of their faces were inches apart at the opening. Eventually, they managed to get nice and snug in the sleeping bag and lay back on the chair. They rested quietly as they gazed up at the stars and the full moon.

Chapter 12 – Revelation under a Full Moon

An owl, not visible but perched in a tree, about two hundred feet away, hooted as Justin and Kelsey lay together on the old, reclining patio chair and wrapped together in Kelsey's sleeping bag. While it was difficult for them to get comfortable, Kelsey was clearly delighted to not be alone, and with both of them still naked, Justin acquiesced to the situation. They were out in the open on Kelsey's ground level patio, and though they were being directly hit by the light reflected off the full moon, they felt hidden by the darkness.

It was a warmer night by Spruce Creek valley standards, but the temperature was still a crisp forty-five degrees. As they gazed straight ahead, to the southwest, toward Riley Ridge in the distance where they had been on their bikes only a few hours ago, a slight breeze picked up and was enough to rustle a small pile of leaves collected in the corner of Kelsey's patio. With only a modest amount of light pollution in the Colorado mountains, many stars can usually be seen.

"I do love the quiet," Justin said in a hushed tone to not disturb Kelsey's neighbors who were all assuredly asleep but had their windows open. "The peace and quiet might be the main reason why I live here," he added.

"Mm-hmm," Kelsey moaned, snuggling up closer to him.

"So is that Kyle's place over there?" Justin asked, motioning his head toward the corner of the next building that was off to the left and on the other side of a grassy open area and a small ditch.

"Yeah," Kelsey muttered, curtly.

The living room and bedroom of Kyle's unit were dark, as with all the other condos around them, but Kyle's windows faced Kelsey's patio. Justin was pensive as he gazed at Kyle's place. Kelsey lay, relaxed and warm, and looked up at the full moon. "Whitney could be looking up at that same moon at this very moment," she said softly, "dreaming of you right now."

"I can assure you she's not thinking of me. Actually, I can assure you she doesn't ever think of me." Kelsey turned her head and softly pressed her cheek against his ear. "I had a star named after her," Justin said.

"What? What are you talking about?"

"There are these websites you can go to and assign names to specific stars." Kelsey looked into his eyes with a wistful smile as he continued, "It's nothing official. It's kind of a joke. Astronomists and governments and professional organizations don't recognize the names, but you can do it for fun. The commercial outfits give you this whole care package with a certificate and a sky chart with the location of the star delineated. One night, when I was thinking about her, I went online and I did it. I still have the certificate."

"Does she know?"

"No."

"Oh," Kelsey groaned, "Justin, Justin, Justin." She relaxed back and looked up at the stars. "Which one's Whitney?"

"You can't see her now. At this time of year, from this location in the hemisphere, you can only see her before dawn. It's a very faint star. You would need a telescope, a good telescope."

"Well, it's sweet. When I was a little girl, my brother taught me all about the constellations."

"Whitney's in the area of Orion."

"Got it. I remember that one."

The wind picked up and was loud as it blew through the surrounding forest, but they were toasty in Kelsey's sleeping bag and shielded from the gusts. As the wind kept blowing, Kelsey shifted her arm to secure a better hug on Justin. One gust was so powerful that a metal chair flipped over on another patio fifty feet away. Looking up at the stars, their thoughts wandered.

They lay silent for a couple minutes as they waited for the wind to die down, and then Kelsey said, "Did you know the word planet comes from the Latin word *planeta*, meaning wanderer, since the planets seem to wander about the night sky relative to the stars?"

"Kelsey!"

"What?"

"Nothing." Justin squeezed her tightly and cocked his head to look into her eyes. "Did you love Brandon?"

"No," Kelsey brusquely replied.

"Huh," Justin uttered to himself. He had a hold of her left hand and was feeling it with his fingers. He could feel her calluses, above her pinkie finger and above her thumb. He could feel again how the calluses arced to match her bite. Kelsey looked around at the night and let her thoughts drift again. Justin pulled her hand up and kissed her calluses gently. He then slowly pulled himself up slightly and whispered into her ear, "Kelsey, you're done biting yourself, okay? No more."

"Okay," she curtly muttered.

"So, I noticed something else when we were on the sofa in there. Kelsey, you're so strong, but I've determined that a lot of your strength comes from tension that builds up inside you as you dwell on the past and things that happened, things that were said. You clench up, full of rage, and you do it so much that your body is a solid rock." Kelsey wiggled in the sleeping bag in another futile effort to get comfortable. "Kelsey, I don't know if I can help you with those thoughts. Maybe nobody can, but you have to figure out a way to let it go and relax, focus on your bright future, if you seize it."

"Okay," she bluntly replied. "Why are you helping me? Why does Hannah want to help me?"

"We truly believe in you. We understand that everything you're sorting through is profoundly real, but in the end though, all we can do is help. It's ultimately up to you to make the needed changes."

"What about all the stuff you're sorting through? Are you going to make the needed changes?" Justin smiled and squeezed Kelsey.

"I'm serious. You need to let some stuff go. I need to know that you've moved on from your nadir of sorrow and that you've stopped wallowing in your toxic gloom."

"Fair enough."

"No, I'm serious. It's okay to be shy, Justin. It's okay to introverted. I realize that your personality will never change, but you've got this ice wall around yourself. You have to let it go. Don't let any of it fester any longer. Quit worrying about what happened in the past. Quit worrying about getting rejected or getting hurt. Justin, if there's anything you take away from here tonight, you're not going to languish any longer. You're going to pick a girl and ask her out." Justin was still. Kelsey whipped her head around and looked into his eyes.

"Okay," he whispered. "This is on you, though. You told me to do it."

Kelsey responded with a firm nod and settled back. Justin nuzzled up to her as she looked at the full moon again. "I used to become so entranced by full moons," she said. "You know, they can help engender such beautiful, spiritual visions. I also thought that man in the moon was going to look after my brother in Iraq and protect him."

"Oh Kelsey, again, I am so sorry."

"I no longer believe the man in the moon cares about me."

"Kelsey, I promise you that man in the moon loves you. I'm not trying to be silly. You are loved. I promise." Justin started caressing Kelsey's hip. "Hey, listen, you are so smart and so strong and so beautiful. Kelsey, you can't ever think of disappearing on us ever again. You would leave so many people behind that would be so hurt for so long. You have to understand that. You can't do that to them. Even that man in the moon would suddenly develop a sad face."

"Do you think anyone will love me the way you loved Whitney?" Justin became still. "Maybe that man in the moon knows," Kelsey went on, "and is looking down on my man right now."

"He is. I mean, somebody does love you."

Kelsey scoffed and rolled her eyes. Staring at Justin, incredulously, she hesitated and then firmly asked, "Who?" Justin lay still. Kelsey wriggled in the sleeping bag, shifting her body so she could look right at his face. "Justin, I'm scared to ask, but who?"

"That's what I was trying to tell you earlier, when we were on the sofa."

"Who?" she barked, causing Justin to shush her as he looked around at the nearby open windows. He glanced back at her and then tilted his head toward Kyle's place. Kelsey turned her head in the same direction. Her breath hitched before she chuckled. "No, no, Justin, he's just a nice guy. He likes to look out for me, but we are so different." Justin shook his head and motioned his head toward Kyle's place again. "Justin," Kelsey blurted out. "Stop it. I promise you, you're wrong about this."

"These past couple weeks, everywhere we've been, he's been there. When you're at the North Fork, he's always sitting at the bar, watching over you through the corner of his eye."

"He's always there."

"No, no, no. He's only there when you're there. When we hiked up to Mount Preston, he was in front of us the entire time, looking back at you, watching your progress, and waiting for you at the top. When we rode up Riley Ridge, he was behind us and I suspect he followed us back down, making sure you made it home okay. How often does he stop by your job sites to talk to Drew?"

"Justin, stop it. He's a plumber, he works on the same projects."

"Kelsey, I know he was the one that saved you last winter when you thought you were going to disappear on us." Kelsey slid down in the sleeping bag, dropping her chin. Justin remained stolid as she whimpered and nuzzled up to him. "When did Kyle move in over there?" Kelsey, with her eyes now barely out of the sleeping bag, peered over at Kyle's bedroom window. "I'll bet," Justin continued, "it was shortly after you moved in here, right?"

"He's stalking me?"

"No, Kelsey, no. I hate that. He's not stalking you. In fact, I would suggest that if he has one redeeming quality it's that he would never ever do anything to hurt you and would never let anyone else hurt you." Justin inhaled deeply and added in a breathy voice, "He wouldn't …because he's hopelessly and desperately in love with you."

Kelsey scoffed and shuffled in the sleeping bag as she tried to sit up. After a few seconds of wrestling with the bag and with Justin's help, they both managed to sit up. Kelsey sighed and slouched. The sleeping bag had become unzipped and Justin was grabbing it and working to hold it up to cover her and keep them warm. After Justin finally got the bag pulled up and wrapped around them, he held still, grasping the sleeping bag in his hand. "He told you this?" Kelsey asked.

"No, I've never talked to Kyle before, but it's so obvious. I suspect the whole valley has witnessed the same behavior and would agree. Kelsey, this is what I was trying to tell you inside. You might have an opportunity, right there, to experience some deep, abiding love, but you've chosen to hang out with a bunch of frickin' losers instead." Justin gritted his teeth and jerked his head back and forth in restrained fury. Kelsey shook her head in disagreement. "I can tell you this," Justin went on, "Kyle has no intention of ever letting you out of his sight." Kelsey sat still. Her head was down, but she was peering up, looking at Kyle's bedroom window.

"He's watching us now?" she whispered.

"I doubt he's looking through the blinds at us at this moment, but I'm sure he's perfectly aware that you're home and I'm here with you."

Justin leaned his head down against Kelsey's shoulder as she sat still, looking over at Kyle's window. Justin could feel goose bumps arising on Kelsey's skin as she suddenly gasped. Justin pulled back. He saw her face blanch in the moonlight as her breath hitched. She raised her hand and covered her mouth. "Justin," she blurted out in a whisper, turning her head. "Oh my gosh, Justin." Justin looked at her curiously. "Oh Justin," she said again dropping her head against her hand. "He was there."

"Where?"

"That night in Vegas. Oh my gosh, Justin, why was he there?" The sleeping bag slipped from Justin's grasp and he worked to pull it up again. "Justin, that Sunday morning, in Vegas, I woke up in our hotel room and I had no idea what happened the night before or how I got back there."

"Oh," Justin droned, "Kelsey, Kelsey, Kelsey."

"No, Justin, I now remember. Everything came to me, just now. I remember everything so vividly. He was there."

"Who did you go to Vegas with?" Kelsey slouched and stared at Justin with a blank look. "Oh right," Justin groaned, "your boys."

"No, Justin, we were at one of those off-strip casinos that have the cheaper tables. I met this other guy there and I was hanging out with him for several hours. My boys left. They went to a strip club. Anyway, I got pretty messed up with this other guy."

"Kelsey, Kelsey, Kelsey," Justin droned again.

"No, Justin, I now remember waking up at that casino. I had passed out in one of the chairs at one of the slot machines. When I woke up, two casino security guards were standing over me, asking me all these questions. I was so wasted, I couldn't talk. All of a sudden, there's Kyle. I remember he talked to the security guards for a while. Our identifications showed that we were both from the same town and he convinced the security guards that I was with him and he would get me back to my room. Justin, he already knew where I was staying. He put me in a cab and we both rode back to my room." Kelsey hesitated. She put her hand over her mouth and looked toward Kyle's bedroom window.

"And?"

"Well, he made me drink a bunch of water and helped me get dressed for bed. I remember, after he helped me to bed, he kissed me, before he left. I think he said it. No, actually, I'm certain he told me that he loved me that night right after he kissed me." A frost fell over Kelsey's face and her mouth was agape. She stared over at Kyle's window, and after a few seconds, she shook her head vigorously. "I never saw him again while I was there."

"He probably saw you."

Tears welled up in Kelsey's eyes as she looked at Justin. "Justin," she purred.

"Kelsey, my back is killing me. Can we lie back?"

They both lay back slowly and looked up at the stars. As they lay quietly, Justin tugged on Kelsey, pulling her toward him, but she didn't respond. She turned her head to look at Kyle's bedroom window again, and Justin conceded and lay back with his face resting on her shoulder. Kelsey suddenly shrieked as a red fox came around the corner of her building and scampered onto the patio. Justin yelped in a whisper and gestured for the fox to scram, which seemed to have the opposite effect, but after Justin wiggled his legs aggressively, the fox trotted away, nimbly.

"Kelsey, you may need to protect me from Kyle." Kelsey didn't respond. "I'm serious. He already thinks I'm maladjusted. Seriously, if needed, I'm trusting you'll step in. He's big."

"Okay." Kelsey chortled. "Justin, he may be more scared of you."

"Right," he replied, dubiously. Justin flinched as he looked up at the sky. "Oh my gosh," he said, quickly motioning his head to the right. Kelsey gasped too as they watched a meteor race across the sky.

Kelsey settled back again. "Justin, I'm done."

"With what?" he asked, turning his head, looking into the whites of her eyes.

"Boys, messing around, getting plastered, all of it. I'm serious." Justin groaned and looked away. Kelsey glared at him. "Justin, I'm serious."

"Okay but know that you have to prove it. Kelsey, I've heard people declare they were going to quit smoking when they were holding a burning cigarette in their hand, at that very moment."

"Justin, I'm serious. I'm done."

"Okay, I'm sorry to say this, but you really have to prove it. I know you're harboring a lot of deplorable memories and can't stand being alone with your thoughts, and that's also why I ended up here tonight. It's part of the reason why we ended up on the sofa together, but you have to accept the memories. Whatever they are. Whatever those boys did when you were messed up. Brandon. Your family. Your brother. Whatever. You also have to find comfort in being alone at times …with all of it. When you want to escape by getting sloshed or messing around, you have to resist that easy out. And, know that you may have to fight some of it for the rest of your life. I promise that I believe in you, but it won't be easy and you have to commit to it like you've never committed to anything in your entire life."

Kelsey lay back and gazed up at the sky. After a couple seconds, she softly said, "Okay." Justin squeezed her and pulled her toward him a couple times, but Kelsey didn't respond. She rolled to her side, as possible in the sleeping bag, and stared at Kyle's bedroom window.

Chapter 12 – Revelation under a Full Moon

Chapter 13 – New Accord for a Bright Future

While overcast and windy that Sunday afternoon, it was warm and dry, providing fine conditions for all in the valley to get out and enjoy another beautiful summer day before the short Spruce Creek summer is over. Somewhat weary from their Saturday bike ride, Adam, Hannah, Josh, and Emily chose to enjoy a quiet break at the North Fork Tavern and were seated at their usual table, dressed casual as they each enjoyed their favorite beverage of late and monitored the televised Rockies baseball game. Cody lay in his regular spot on the sidewalk. Adam and Josh commented on the status of the baseball game as Hannah and Emily skimmed separate copies of the Spruce Creek News.

Two servers were working that afternoon, attending separately to three families seated for lunch and two girls, new resort employees, that were seated together. Music was faintly playing, but the volume was so low, it was difficult to make out the songs. Light collective laughter suddenly erupted at the bar causing Hannah to peer over. As she turned her head, she noticed Kyle. He was sitting with two other regular locals and talking football with the tavern owner, Jake. A stream of expletives suddenly rumbled from the other end of the tavern where two of Kelsey's boys were playing pool.

The door to the tavern opened and it was quiet enough that the squeak could be heard across the restaurant. Emily nudged Josh. Justin, carrying a book along with a new pool cue, walked in. He was moving swiftly, as normal, but progressed with some additional zest, walking more upright and shoulders back. He strolled straight over to Jake and handed him the pool cue. Justin pursed his lips as he paused, awaiting a response. Jake smacked him firmly on the back and Justin proceeded to his usual table in the back right near the foosball table and the wood stove. Justin certainly had a glow about him, but before sitting down, he noticed Kelsey's boys playing pool and a feral snarl descended over his face. He instantly looked away. Kelsey's boys had to have heard him growl, but they chose to ignore him.

"Justin," Josh called. "Really? You're not even going to say hi."

"I'm going to go talk to him," Hannah said as she got up and proceeded to his table. Justin, with his right leg already up on his left knee and reading his book, shifted nervously in his seat as Hannah sat in the chair opposite him. She slowly put her right elbow on the table and rested her chin in her hand as she gazed into his eyes. "Everything good?" she asked, sweetly, blinking her eyes playfully.

"As far as I know."

"Do you want to tell me about it?" Justin hesitated for a couple seconds. As a grin emerged, he shook his head, wiggling his body slightly. "What are you reading?" Justin's eyes got real big and he slammed the book closed, pulling it under the table. Hannah started grinning. "Wait a second," she said, chuckling. She stood up and stepped around the table. "No, no, no, what are you reading?" With her right hand on his shoulder, she reached down, and with her left hand, she gently pulled his arm. He didn't resist. It was a D.H. Lawrence novel. "Justin," she yelled.

"What?" He said, dropping his head. "I thought I might learn something," he added with his voice trailing off.

Hannah stood smiling as he slowly opened the book again. "Okay," she said, "well, come join us in a bit and we'll talk about your journal paper, okay? We both read it." Justin nodded. Hannah leaned down and coquettishly whispered into his ear, "Thanks again for checking on Kelsey last night, okay?"

"Uh, yeah," Justin said tensely but with excitement. "Anytime." Hannah watched him for a couple seconds. Her eyes gradually narrowed as she walked back to her seat.

As Hannah returned to her seat, Adam and Emily were smiling. Hannah didn't get a chance to comment before Josh grabbed Emily's arm and said, "Look at this," motioning back toward Justin. "Can you explain this to me?" The two girls who had been sitting together were now standing next to Justin, giggling. Both were round-eyed with light complexions and long, dark hair pulled back in pony tails. They could have passed as sisters. Justin wasn't as nervous as usual and visibly reveled over their attention. Emily turned toward Hannah, and they both tittered. "Seriously," Josh said, holding out his hands with palms up as he looked at Adam. "Girls see him hanging out with Kelsey a few times and talking to Hannah and now they're envious. That's it. Nothing else has changed."

"Maybe they saw him break that pool cue," Adam said.

"Are you jealous?" Emily asked, batting her eyelashes as she gazed into Josh's eyes.

Josh dropped his head. "No," he mumbled, "I'll just never get women." Hannah grinned. Emily put her arm around Josh and gently pulled on him.

They all watched Justin for a minute as he talked to his new friends and smiled and fidgeted nervously in his seat. The door squeaked again. It was Kelsey's roommate, Sadie. She walked straight toward Hannah. "Hannah," she blurted out in a shrill scream. "What did you do?"

"What?" Hannah replied, bemused and startled over the inquisition.

"Kelsey cleaned up the entire apartment this morning." Hannah cracked an uncontrollable smile as she looked at Adam and dropped her head against his shoulder. "When I walked in this morning, I thought Adam may have been there again, but I went to the bathroom and Kelsey was scrubbing the tub!" Emily burst out laughing. "Seriously Hannah, I don't understand." Sadie grabbed a stool from the adjacent high top and sat at the end of the table. "You know, Hannah, I tried last spring."

"I know," Hannah said softly, nodding.

Sadie looked at Adam. "I gave her some serious doses of tough love, but nothing ever took." Sadie looked back at Hannah. "What did you do?"

Hannah smiled and motioned her head toward Justin. Sadie looked at Justin who was still talking to his new friends. Sadie, with her brow furrowed, whipped her head back toward Hannah. "It was Adam's idea," Hannah said, smiling uncontrollably. "I was skeptical, but Justin's helped. He really has. He's had a strange, unique influence on her."

The door squeaked and Emily gasped. She was slapping her hand on the table. It was Kelsey. Josh glared at Emily and implored, "Would you calm down?" Kelsey was dolled up, wearing makeup, and her hair was pulled back and smooth over her head. She was donning a snug, white, short-sleeve top with frills around the neck and strings at the end of the sleeves. Her top was short and tight around her belly, exposing her belly button, and she had on tight, black jeans and black ankle booties.

The mood in the tavern immediately became imbued with Kelsey's allure, even more than normal, and while everyone was distracted, it didn't have any effect on her. Justin peered around the two girls at his table and watched Kelsey as she marched fluidly toward Sadie. Kelsey didn't even look at her boys playing pool. The two girls with Justin were clearly perturbed with the attention he gave Kelsey.

When Kelsey approached Sadie, she hugged her and kissed her flush on the lips. Sadie pulled back, but she had long ago become accustomed to Kelsey's affections. Kelsey whispered something into Sadie's ear. "We're good," Sadie replied as she caressed Kelsey's back. "Everything's fine."

Kelsey stepped around Adam, dragging her hand over his shoulders, and then gave Hannah a hug. "Hey sweetie," Hannah said, accepting Kelsey's embrace. Hannah, with her chin on Kelsey's shoulder, looked at Adam. Even if Hannah wanted to, she wouldn't have been able to get rid of her uncontrollable smile. Kelsey slowly stood back and sighed as she looked into Hannah's green eyes. "Well aren't you all dolled up this afternoon," Hannah said. "What's the occasion that has you looking so winsome and beautiful?"

Kelsey didn't respond. She patted Hannah delicately on the head and then turned to look toward the bar. Josh and Adam immediately shifted in their seats to look in the same direction. Kelsey was staring right at Kyle and quickly became transfixed. Sadie and Emily also looked in the same direction. They were all speechless as they looked around at each other.

Attempting to end the awkward silence, Josh asked Adam, "So did you finish Justin's paper?" Kelsey continued to stare at Kyle and leaned back against Hannah.

"Yeah," Adam replied. Hannah was nodding too. "We both read it this morning as we made pancakes."

Hannah perked up in her seat and said, "Silver iodide," in reference to Justin's paper on cloud seeding.

"The resort's doing this now?" Josh asked.

"Yeah," Adam started as he looked toward Hannah for support, "so the resort hired a contractor to set up and operate some ground-based generators that burn a solution, releasing silver iodide particles into the air. The generators are down the valley, to the northwest. When there's weather moving in and saturated clouds are moving up the valley – and other criteria are met - the generators are fired up. They're controlled remotely and spray plumes of silver iodide particles into the clouds."

"Yeah, yeah," Hannah interjected, "so, the supercooled water vapor in the clouds is attracted to the silver iodide particles and the vapor freezes into ice, or snow."

"Justin analyzed a bunch of data and did some modeling," Adam droned on.

Emily and Sadie weren't listening to Adam and Hannah. They were still focused on Kelsey who was leaning back against Hannah's side and engrossed by Kyle. Hannah awkwardly moved her left arm around Kelsey's hips to help support her, and while it would appear that Hannah would be uncomfortable and distracted, she remained enthralled in the discussion about Justin's paper. "Justin included a whole slew of charts in his paper," she said.

"Anyway," Adam added, "he found that there is a loose trend which indicates that there may be as much as a ten percent increase in snowfall from a particular storm when the cloud seeding generators are running, but he also emphasizes that more data are needed to reach a definitive conclusion. He documents that the effectiveness is difficult to isolate because for a particular cloud seeding application during a given storm, it is of course not known how much precipitation would have been realized without the cloud seeding."

"Okay, so my understanding," Josh said, "is that even if there is only a tenuous relationship between cloud seeding and increased snowfall, the resort is going to continue with it. I mean, why wouldn't they if there is any chance at a ten percent increase in snowfall, right?"

Adam hesitated as he looked over toward Justin. "Well," he said, "we could call Justin over here to discuss it further, but..." Adam paused and smiled. He shook his head playfully as he watched Justin talking to the same two girls. "I guess we'll leave him alone for now." Josh smiled as he nodded.

Kelsey suddenly stood up, startling everyone. She took a deep breath, and without saying anything, started walking toward the bar. There was something different about her movement that not only attracted attention, but drew a hush over the tavern. She wasn't moving with her signature plod but was moving with a certain elegance and newfound refinement in her steps. The two servers, who had been moving about, were also debilitated by her fluid movement, and even the three families from out of town were captivated and stopped chewing their food as they watched her ease between their tables. Kelsey's boys stood still at the pool table. Justin stopped talking, mid-sentence, and leaned to his side to see around his two new friends.

Kelsey walked right up to Kyle and sat in an empty stool to his right. She didn't speak for several seconds as she sat, perpendicular to the bar and facing him. The audio from a couple televisions could suddenly be heard due to the hush by the patrons. Kyle sat easy. He didn't turn, but his eyes shifted toward her. Kelsey stood up, slowly put her arms around him, and began talking softly into his ear.

Her comments were inaudible, and light conversations gradually ensued again. Kelsey's boys refocused on their game of pool but were mumbling expletives as they shook their heads and waved their hands at Kelsey. Kyle, showing no emotion, gazed down at the bar as he listened intently to Kelsey's whispers. When she eventually stopped, she grabbed him, nuzzled up to him, and held him. He slowly put his arms around her. They talked softly for another minute before standing and moving to an empty table. Kelsey sat to his left, close to him, her left knee cleaved between his knees. He slid his right arm down on the table and leaned his head against his hand. Kelsey leaned forward and her face was only inches away from his as he stared back into her eyes. He grabbed her hand and spoke softly.

Kelsey's boys suddenly threw their pool cues on the table and stormed out of the tavern. Kelsey didn't even look at them or flinch as they exited. Hannah started giggling. She was clapping her hands together but trying not to make any noise. She leaned over and hugged Adam. Hannah's eyes became locked on Justin, who was now sitting by himself and emotionless as he stared at Kelsey and Kyle.

Emily's eyes followed Hannah's eyes. "Oh boy," Emily said, "guys, see, I told you to be careful. Josh, do something." Josh got up and walked over to Justin's table, and after a quick exchange, they both walked back together.

"Hi Justin," Hannah said, sprightly.

"Hello," Justin said as he stood somewhat eerily off to Sadie's side.

"You know anything about this?" Adam asked, motioning toward Kelsey and Kyle. Justin replied with a whimsical shrug.

"You okay?" Hannah asked.

"I'm fine."

Hannah stood up and stepped around Adam to give Justin a hug. "Justin," she whispered, "again, thank you so much."

"It looks like you're going to have to find another girl for him now," Josh said.

"Oh," Hannah said, as she pulled back from her embrace and rubbed his arm. "Justin's going to be fine."

"So what was up with her yesterday?" Adam asked. "When we're were talking about Sunnis versus Shias."

"Oh no," Sadie interjected as her eyes got real big, "you didn't go there, did you?" They all stared at her. "You know about her brother, right?"

Justin whispered to Sadie, "She doesn't want people talking about it."

Sadie shook her head vigorously. "No, no, no," Sadie said, "I made the mistake of talking to her once about the Israeli-Palestinian conflict."

Adam and Josh perked up, causing Emily to roll her eyes. "Oh, I need to hear this," Josh said. "So you're a Zionist, right?"

Sadie exhaled deeply and rolled her eyes. "Yes Josh, I am a Zionist. I believe that Jews deserve a nation of their own." Sadie looked at Emily. They both rolled their eyes again and shook their heads.

"Seriously, help me out with this," Josh said.

Sadie sighed as her eyes drifted down toward the table. Adam got up and grabbed another stool from an adjacent table and pushed it behind Justin. "Sit," Adam commanded.

"Where to start?" Sadie mumbled to herself.

"Speak softly," Justin whispered as he peered over at Kelsey.

Sadie leaned forward and put her elbows on the high top. "Well, the conflict is about land," she started, in a hushed tone. "I guess we could start back when the area was British Palestine, established after World War I. At that time, Jews were allowed to migrate to British Palestine from other areas of the world." Sadie looked at Josh and hesitated as she paused to gather her thoughts. "After World War II, after the Holocaust, that is, surviving Jews obviously needed a place to go. They weren't going to resettle in many of the old areas that had been occupied by Nazis, so more and more Jews migrated to British Palestine. Well, with the subsequent growing strife between the Jews and Arabs in British Palestine, the United Nations divided the region into a separate Jewish state and a separate Arab state, Israel and Palestine. The neighboring Arab states declared war."

"Well, I assume the British bolted at that point," Adam suggested.

"Yep, they were gone," Sadie replied. "Israel won the war, expanding the borders, and left Arab Palestinians with the Gaza Strip, located along the Mediterranean coast in the southern part of the region, and the West Bank, located along the eastern border of the region."

Adam said, "Other countries were receiving a lot Palestinian refugees during that time. I know that."

Hannah smacked him on the arm. "Let her talk," she admonished.

"Of course the conflict continued, and in 1967, Israel expanded its territory further in the Six Days War to include Sinai from Egypt and the Golan Heights from Syria. Israel also took control of the Gaza Strip and the West Bank."

"Speak softly," Justin whispered again as he looked at Kelsey.

"Relax, dude. She can't hear us. Anyway, in 1978, through the Camp David Accords, Sinai was returned to Egypt, but the Gaza Strip and West Bank still remained controlled by Israel."

"I know this next part," Josh interjected. "The Israelis began establishing communities, or settlements, as they're called, in the Gaza Strip and West Bank and those settlements are not recognized internationally."

"Also, even though Israel withdrew from Gaza," Adam added, "they still effectively retained control of that territory."

"Adam," Hannah blurted out as she smacked him again. "Seriously," she added, turning toward Josh, "you two need to learn to listen."

Emily unleashed her own vicious, backhanded smack to Josh's chest. "What the hell?" he exclaimed.

"Hannah," Adam said, "the settlements are a key part of the problem." Sadie scoffed and waved her hand as she leaned back in her seat.

"Justin," Emily said, "you tell us. What's the solution?"

Justin groaned and shook his head as they all looked at him. He clicked his tongue, and as he hesitated, the music in the restaurant could be faintly heard. It was Dreaming by Blondie. A crooked smile descended over his face as he muttered to himself, "What are the odds?" He slowly turned his head toward Kelsey, and their eyes met. They both smiled. Adam, Hannah, Josh, Emily, and Sadie were all looking around at each other with furrowed brows. Justin slowly rotated his head back, stared toward the middle of the high top, and inhaled before letting his smile fade.

"Okay, well, it's not an easy problem," he said, turning back toward Emily. He sighed as he leaned his torso forward. "There does need to be some acceptance that Israel has the right to exist, and any rhetoric to the contrary is not going to yield anything good for anyone."

"Thank you," Sadie yelled as she playfully slapped him on the arm.

"And the violence has to cease," Justin went on. "Until the violence stops, we are stuck at an impasse. Any violence will assuredly derail progress toward any long standing peace." He paused, in thought, as he looked out the window. "Emily, I don't know. There is indeed still an issue with the Palestinian refugees that ended up in other countries during the past struggles."

"Oh," Sadie groaned, "most of those refugees are descendants of earlier refugees, and those younger refugees have now lived in those other countries their entire lives. Those other countries simply need to accept them as their own citizens." Sadie shifted in her seat. She glared at Justin and asked, "What about the Jews from those same other countries that were displaced from those countries during the conflict?"

Justin shrugged. "Israel does need to loosen its control of the Gaza strip," he said, looking at Sadie. Sadie shrugged.

Justin turned back toward Emily and said, "We do know this, the current situation is unsustainable. But we also know that Muslims, Jews, and Christians have lived together, peacefully, in this region of the world before, for long periods of time. It can happen again. With support from the rest of the world, some give and take, some understanding and tolerance, it could happen, but everyone first needs to figure out a way to let events of the past go and figure out a way to let the grudges go."

They all sat quietly for a few seconds before Sadie grumbled, "If I had known I was going to get waylaid over the future of Israel, I can assure you I would never have come in here."

"Sorry," Josh whispered.

Sadie's attention became locked on Kelsey again, and Hannah dropped her head to watch Cody through the window. Adam and Josh looked up at the televised Rockies game.

"So Hannah," Justin blurted out, "when's your due date?"

"What?!" Hannah shrieked.

"Oh Hannah, you are so pregnant."

"Justin," Hannah yelled. "What the–"

"Hannah," Emily screamed with her mouth agape and eyes wide open.

"Emily, I'm not pregnant. Justin, what the–"

"Oh Hannah," Justin said, "for the last two weeks, you've always been drinking water. You're drinking water again now. You were drinking decaffeinated tea at the Java Alley the other day." Justin laughed loudly. "Hannah, you are so knocked up."

"Oh my gosh," Emily screamed, causing the rest of the patrons to turn. "Hannah!" Emily screamed again as she jumped out of her seat and ran around the table to hug her. Hannah shook her head at Justin. Hannah's face became beet red. She looked over at Adam who was trying to maintain his poker face but started to smile, causing a scowl to descend over Josh's face.

"Justin," Hannah said, "I'm going to kill you."

"Oh, it's fine," Adam mumbled. Emily was jumping up and down, gleefully, as she squeezed Hannah.

"Adam," Hannah whispered, "we haven't even told our families yet." Adam waved his hand. Adam glanced over at Josh, but Josh scoffed and looked away toward the televised baseball game. Emily had begun crying and was wiping her eyes. Adam tilted his head and stared at Josh.

"So that's what's been going on with you," Sadie said. "All the brooding and nurturing over Kelsey's situation. Your maternal instincts had already kicked in."

"Justin," Hannah said harshly, "I'm going to kill you."

"Hey," Josh interjected, motioning his head toward the front door. Kyle and Kelsey were walking out together. They all turned to watch.

"Hannah," Sadie yelled, "what is going on here? Kelsey's hanging with Kyle, you're pregnant, and Justin's talking!"

Hannah glared at Justin again, but Justin had turned his head. He was looking at his two new friends who were sitting back at their table. One of the girls waved at him. He took a deep breath, tapped his hand on the table a few times, and slowly walked to their table. He could be heard faintly as he resumed their previous discussion. Adam, Hannah, Josh, Emily, and Sadie were all smiling but silent as they peered over at him. It was quiet enough that they were able to listen as he started talking.

"So anyway," Justin said to his new friends, "back in the mining days, heavy metals such as cadmium and zinc were released into Spruce Creek from the old mines way up in the headwaters. The heavy metals destroyed the ecosystem, but bulkheads were recently added to seal off the mines, and treatment facilities were also set up to remove the heavy metals from the water seeping out of the hillside around the mine. With that work, the ecosystem is improving. Also, in addition to the mayflies and caddisflies in the river, giant stoneflies have been reintroduced. With the overall improvements to the ecosystem, brown trout and rainbow trout populations are coming back to Spruce Creek." Adam, Hannah, Josh, Emily, and Sadie were all smiling at each other.

"Oh boy," Emily mumbled.

Chapter 13 – New Accord for a Bright Future

Chapter 14 – Plea for Universal Awareness

Leaves rustled on the four mature aspen clustered to the left of the front door at the Java Alley as Adam, Hannah, Josh, and Emily, all dressed for their workday, sat on the brick patio, around a small, iron table that was centered in front of the large window to the coffee shop. It was early that Wednesday morning and the mass of summer tourists that would eventually take over the resort plaza had not arrived yet. Other businesses in the plaza were still closed. The sun had risen above the mountains to the east, and Josh and Emily could feel the sun on their backs as Adam and Hannah had their chairs positioned perfectly to feel the warm rays on their faces. Cody, sitting next to Adam, was captivated by a young black Labrador playing in the middle of the plaza, though Cody remained calm as Adam twirled his ear.

Every time the door to the shop opened, they could hear the whirr of the coffee roaster and the aroma of freshly roasted Kona beans would waft over them. The door opened yet again, squeaking and drowning out the reggae music emanating softly from two speakers posted above the large window to the shop. Cody immediately turned his head and watched as Britt walked out with all their drinks.

As Emily received her latte, she softly asked Britt, "Hey, is Justin in there?"

"In his usual spot," Britt replied.

"I'll get him," Josh said.

As Josh scurried inside, Emily looked at Hannah and asked, "How's he doing?" Hannah shrugged. Emily inhaled and turned to Adam. "Has he talked to her?"

"I don't think so," Adam responded.

Hannah smiled and said, "I think she and Kyle have spent every moment together since Sunday." Hannah looked at Adam and asked, "Has she been showing up for work at all?"

"Nope. She called Drew and asked if she could have a few days off. It sounded like she was very genuine with her request and assured Drew she was finally sorting through some stuff."

Josh walked back out and plopped down in his iron chair. The legs of the chair rubbed loudly on the brick patio, one step above the asphalt that covered the plaza. Justin stepped out of the shop, moving slowly, seeming somewhat despondent. "Hey Justin," Hannah said sprightly as he walked out. Justin nodded politely. He stepped around all of them and sat at the adjacent table, with his back to the coffee shop window. "How are you?" Hannah asked, somewhat whimsically.

"Hannah," Justin replied, brusquely, "I have a story for you." Hannah wiggled her eyebrows as she looked at Adam and then Emily. Justin cleared his throat. "Okay," he started, "so, do you know Erin?"

"Uh, the hostess at the steakhouse?"

"Yeah, do you know her?"

"Nah. I mean, I know who she is."

"So I go in there on occasion, and I'll say hi to her, if I get an opportunity." Josh and Adam were grinning. "Last night, I said hello to her again, and I guess I was being a little more enthusiastic than usual. I really tried to talk to her."

"Justin," Josh interjected, chuckling, "you never would have done that before."

"Oh boy," Emily said, shaking her head, "it's official. Justin's unhinged."

"No, I'm not the one who's gone mad," Justin retorted, staring at Emily. "She called the police on me."

186

"What?!" Hannah shrieked. A scowl descended over Josh's face.

"Yeah, I was only asking her about how her summer was going. I know I didn't talk to her for more than a couple minutes. I believe I was being perfectly pleasant. After it became clear that she wasn't into it, I went over and sat at the bar. About fifteen minutes later this cop walks up to me and asks if he can talk to me outside."

"I told you guys," Emily said. "I told you. I told you early on that you were playing with fire. I knew somebody was going to get hurt in this whole deal." Josh, with his face turning beet red and his teeth grinding, whipped his head around and stared at Emily.

"Anyway," Justin went on, "so I'm outside there at the steakhouse, talking to this cop, and he's questioning me and checking me out as if I'm some sort of psychotic stalker. The other employees didn't want to have anything to do with it, and I overheard the manager telling Erin that she started this and it was her deal. I admitted to the cop that I may have been a little fervent in my interaction with her. Gosh, I had to go on defense. I emphasized that I had never touched her or followed her or tried to track her down. I never asked her out or called her or even asked for her number."

"Oh Justin," Hannah said. "I'm so sorry."

Emily scoffed and sniped, "Justin, you probably were being a total weirdo."

"So?" Adam asked, looking at Justin..

"Well, I actually had a good time talking to this cop. I told him about my background and what I do. We also talked about life being single in Spruce Creek and chicks. I opened up to this guy about everything. I guess I felt like I had to. I told him about everything I've been through over the past couple weeks with Kelsey. Of course he knew Kelsey. I even told him about the broken pool cue." Adam's eyes got real big as Josh chuckled. "So Erin walks out and sees me laughing with this cop and boy, she got mad. She went back in, slamming the door and storming around, sputtering expletives, making a ruckus however she could. All the employees were rolling their eyes at her."

"Good grief," Josh said. "You see, one guy shows a little interest in her, but she's so confident that she is so out of his league that she becomes offended, and she is so offended that he would even think she could be interested in him, that she tries to have the guy arrested."

"Yes!" Justin yelled. "Exactly. Thank you."

"Alright, so what happened?" Hannah asked.

"So the cop and I meet with the manager and Erin, and the cop says he's got nothing to act on and he's talked to me and is confident that I won't bother her again. I offered to never go there again, but the manager dismissed that, and oh, that made Erin seethe even more. But then," Justin hesitated as he started chuckling, "the cop whispers to Erin, 'Are you sure you don't want to go out with this guy?'" Hannah, Adam, Josh, and Emily busted out in hysterical laughter. Justin laughed too as he tried to continue. "Yeah, the manager was giggling under his breath."

"Oh Justin," Hannah droned.

"I'm not done. It gets better. I go back in. I had already ordered food. My food was there and getting cold. So I'm chatting with the bartender and a couple other employees come over there and try to make me feel better and tell me Erin's an idiot."

"See," Josh interjected, looking at Emily, "Justin sees that she's not dating anyone, and he figures, I'll try to talking to her, but the whole reason she's not dating anyone is because she thinks she's too good for anyone."

Emily was shaking her head. She blurted out, "I'm sorry, but, Justin, you can be such a weirdo. I'm not surprised by any of this."

"The cop left," Justin went on, looking at Adam and Hannah, "and the attention of the employees and patrons finally shifted away from me. I relaxed and ate my steak."

"Good for you for staying," Josh blurted out.

"So I'm talking about bumble bees and cloud seeding and stuff with the bartender, and Erin comes over and sits by me."

Adam busted out in laughter again as Josh threw up his hands. Hannah was smiling as she looked at Emily who was shaking her head.

Adam managed to stifle his laughter enough to say, "I'm surprised you're telling us about this."

"Well, I figured you would hear about it anyway. There were a lot of people there watching it all go down. So all the patrons and employees were staring again."

"Good grief," Josh howled.

"Wait, I'm still not done. So, Erin and I talked for fifteen minutes or so. She was cold, but I've been in a weird place after these last few days and I believe I did an okay job getting her to warm up to me. The bartender helped me. It turns out she has a degree in biology from Colorado State. Anyway, we're going out tomorrow night!" Adam and Josh busted out in raucous laughter again, this time, startling Cody.

"Justin," Hannah yelled, "Erin's so cute."

"Anyway, I'm hoping you might help me out a bit. You know, stop by and say hi for a few minutes at some point." Justin looked at Emily and said, "It might help for Erin to see that I'm not really so much of a weirdo."

"No Justin," Emily said, "you're total weirdo."

"I might try to get that cop to stop by and help me too."

"Man," Adam said, "if you two started dating, what a story you could tell people for years."

"Hey," Josh started, looking at Adam, "no, no, no, this is perfect." Josh shifted forward in his chair and continued, "Justin managed to tame Kelsey. Maybe he can fix Erin too! Break her down and build her back up again."

"Oh," Emily yelled, smacking Josh on the arm, "Erin's fine. I'm telling all of you. There's nothing wrong with her. Justin's the one that needs fixed. I'm sure Erin's had so many aggressive guys approaching her all the time. It's inevitable she would be defensive."

They all sat quietly for a minute, chuckling lightly over Justin's story. Emily suddenly started shushing them and smacking Josh on the arm.

"Why do you do that?" Josh asked. "Would you please stop doing that. Just chill."

Emily was looking toward the other side of the plaza, and Adam and Hannah looked in the same direction. Kelsey and Kyle were walking toward them. They were both dressed nicely and enjoying the attention during what could only be described as a slow promenade through the resort plaza. They certainly attracted the attention of the few others that were in the plaza. Kelsey was bubbly as they walked up, and Kyle progressed briskly around Josh and Emily. He nodded at Adam before stepping into shop. "Hi sweetie," Hannah said to Kelsey.

Kelsey, with her face beaming, walked over and stood behind Hannah. She slowly leaned down and gave Hannah a nice, firm hug. Kelsey reached down and rubbed her hand gently on Hannah's belly and whispered into her ear, "Congratulations." Kelsey then gave Hannah a sensuous kiss on the neck before looking at Adam, and with a big grin, she whispered, "You're so lucky."

"So what's going on?" Hannah said, exuberantly. Kelsey was mum as she stood up and rubbed Hannah's shoulders.

"Well don't you look like the cat that ate the canary?" Emily said. "Come on, sing it, sister."

Kelsey was still quiet as she walked around Josh, messing up his hair, and then sidled up to Emily. Kelsey leaned down, and without hesitation, kissed Emily flush on the lips before Emily could pull away. Emily rolled her eyes and chuckled as she looked over at Josh. Kelsey then stood up and walked over to Justin in her newly acquired elegant movement. She slowly sat in a chair at his table, reached her hand over, and gently rubbed his chest.

"Was I right?" Justin whispered. Kelsey, still smiling and showing her teeth, nodded back. Adam, Hannah, Josh, and Emily were looking at each other quizzically, furrowing their brows. "So," Justin said softly, "you told me to ask somebody out, and I did it."

Kelsey frowned, stuck out her lower lip, and softly said, "I know. I heard. You okay?"

"I guess," Justin said with a shrug.

Kelsey looked right into Justin's eyes as she slowly dropped her hand and began massaging his knee. After a few more seconds of awkwardness, she said, "Adam," while maintaining her gaze on Justin.

"Yes," Adam replied, slowly.

"So what's it all about?"

"What's that?"

Kelsey slowly sat up and took a breath as she said, "All this discourse we've been having about global warming, uranium enrichment, the gold standard, Sunnis and Shias." Holding her hand on Justin's knee, she slowly looked over at Adam. "Kyle was asking me why the heck we've been talking about all this stuff. He asked what's the nexus among all these topics?"

Kyle walked out and kneeled down to pet Cody. "Well," Adam said, "it's all about keeping proper focus." Adam took a deep breath and sat up in his chair before continuing, "Collectively, we do control what politicians do. When we choose leaders and monitor their work, we can focus on the facts behind situations and the salient details about all the critical issues facing our communities, the country, and the world, or we can choose to only pay attention to trivial, inconsequential goings-on."

"And," Josh interjected, "it's important to understand that there are not opposing viewpoints in regards to the science and the proper, technical analyses of the facts of a situation and in regards to the sound, solid evaluations of every issue. People may try to refute the immutable laws of science or refute the facts of a situation, but those are the givens before any potential follow-up policy options are defined and considered."

"We can make efforts on our own," Adam said, "to make sure that we, along with the entire electorate, are cognizant of all the rudimentary details, realities, and key aspects behind major political issues. Policy and decisions need to be developed and refined with careful review of the data and with reference to the years of analyses completed by experts that have spent their entire careers analyzing the data. Policy needs to be developed based on the findings from those efforts as opposed to raw emotions, emotions that run rampant based on fear, greed, and hate and emotions that can so easily become misguided. We as people, the voters, have the ability to assure that smart policy is implemented by educating ourselves first, educating our children, and leading debates in our communities with proper focus on furthering the understanding of basic truths."

Kelsey, with a curious look on her face, turned toward Justin. As his eyes caught hers, he responded, "Facts first, policy later."

"The details are complicated," Josh said as Kelsey swiveled her head back.

"Sure," Adam responded, looking at Kelsey, "but anyone can still have an understanding of the basic facts behind all the problematic situations and issues facing policymakers, and with that foundation, they can choose to properly evaluate the problems on their own and resist the urge to let unchecked emotions, led by an unenlightened mob, dictate how they think, how they vote, and, ultimately, how governmental policy is formulated. Once the electorate becomes educated, they can then hold elected officials accountable and assure policymakers exhibit good judgment, awareness, and acumen when policy decisions are made, but if voters elect representatives based on flawed understanding of the science and the underlying principles of important issues, all the culpability lies with the voters for the subsequent damage done by those elected politicians."

Britt walked out with two drinks. She handed one drink to Kyle and moved anxiously over to Kelsey. As she walked around to Kelsey, Kelsey's expression became cold. Britt sighed as she slowly handed Kelsey her coffee. Kelsey was stiff and frigid. Britt crouched beside her. She looked up into Kelsey's hazel eyes and slowly put her hand on Kelsey's knee. As she gazed up at Kelsey, Kelsey stared blankly toward the ski mountain.

Adam, Hannah, Josh, and Emily were all looking at each other with furrowed brows. Josh, clearly looking to ease the unexplained tension, asked Adam, "Did you see that unassisted triple play last night?" Adam nodded, acknowledging the sports highlight of the night by the Rockies third baseman.

Britt held still. She then put both her hands on Kelsey's knee. "I'm so sorry," she whispered. Kelsey's eyes narrowed. Justin reached out gently and grabbed Kelsey's hand on the table. Kelsey peered over at him without moving her head. Justin looked into her eyes and tilted his head ever so slightly. The tension was so palpable that Cody suddenly stood up and lumbered under the tables toward Kelsey. He weaved around Josh's and Emily's legs and the table legs and nuzzled his head up against Kelsey's leg. Kelsey sighed and rolled her eyes. She put her left hand on Britt's hand. Britt rose up, gave Kelsey a hug, and whispered again, "I'm so sorry." Kelsey put her arm around Britt as Britt kissed her on the cheek. Britt held her for several seconds before she finally pulled away. Quickly wiping a tear away, Britt scurried back inside. Adam held both his hands out with palms up. He looked at Justin, but Justin shrugged and took a sip of his coffee.

"Alright Adam," Justin said, ineffectively trying to imitate Adam's voice, "so how do we assure everyone is knowledgeable about the facts behind the problematic situations and the issues facing policymakers and assure that the key findings from proper technical analyses are considered? How do we assure that good decisions are subsequently made and that sound, appropriate policies are ultimately implemented?"

Adam sighed as he watched Cody slowly lumber out toward the middle of the plaza. "I don't know," he groaned. "I really don't know." Adam grinned as he looked toward Josh and whimsically added, "I'm working on figuring that out."

Kyle stood up and walked over to sit in the chair beside Kelsey. Kelsey promptly reached over and put her arm around his shoulders. "So," Kelsey said as she looked at Kyle, "we have some news."

Hannah and Emily froze. They became wide-eyed as they slowly raised their heads and stared at Kelsey and then over at Kyle. Justin was frozen too as he gazed down at the table. Kelsey looked at Kyle, and he smiled and raised his eyebrows before inhaling through his teeth. Emily gasped and peered over at Hannah. Hannah reached over and grabbed Adam's arm, and Adam gritted his teeth as he sat up in his seat.

"I'm going to go back to Texas for the fall," Kelsey said. Adam, Hannah, Josh, and Emily all exhaled deeply. "I'm going to finish my degree," Kelsey added. Josh took a breath and slouched in his seat as Kelsey looked over at Hannah and added, "Kyle's going to go with me. My cousin's working on some spec houses and has a few months of plumbing work for him. I'm hoping I can graduate in December. We're leaving on Friday. Sadie's going to move back into our place and her beau's going to sublet the remainder of my portion of the lease. His lease is up at the end of the month."

"Kelsey," Hannah said, "that is so great."

Justin was smiling. He looked down at Kelsey's hand, resting softly on the table, next to his drink, and he noticed the calluses on her hand had softened and were healing. He tilted his head slightly toward her. She could see his eyes had begun to water. She stood up, her chair rubbing against Kyle's chair and catching the attention of Cody who was now in the middle of the plaza. "Come here," Kelsey whispered to Justin as she pulled him up. They hugged each other, close, and Justin nuzzled Kelsey as they continued to hold each other.

Emily sighed and blurted out, "Well, we have some news too." Emily turned toward Josh. "Josh got the job."

"The condo complex?" Hannah yelled.

"Yep," Emily responded. "Also," Emily said, taking a breath, "we're closing on a lot in your subdivision. We already got approved for a construction loan."

"Oh my goodness," Hannah yelled.

"Which lot?" Adam asked.

"One-forty-three," Josh promptly replied. "On the other side of the drainage pond–"

"Yeah, I know the one," Adam said.

"Don't worry," Emily said, "we're not going to be popping in all the time, but you're going to have new neighbors! Hopefully by the end of next summer."

"Does anyone know a good architect?" Josh asked with a half-smile as he peered over at Adam.

Hannah turned and looked at Adam. "I might know one," she said sweetly.

Kelsey finally released her grasp on Justin and they both sat. Kelsey looked back at Kyle and put her hand on his knee. "Let me know if you need a plumber," she said.

"Do you think Drew will help with the landscaping?" Emily asked Adam.

"He will," Hannah interjected. "He might see it as an opportunity to work on Josh's politics."

"Well, speaking of architecture," Adam said, "I got to go to work."

"Yeah," Josh said, as they all began to stand up, "me too. We're contracted for the first delivery to the new condos in two weeks."

"Yeah, we need to pack," Kelsey uttered.

They all strolled into the plaza in different directions, except for Adam and Hannah who got caught in an embrace.

"Thank you so much," Hannah whispered in his ear. She started to tear up, "Adam, thank you so much." They squeezed each other and she added, "See you tonight."

Chapter 14 – Plea for Universal Awareness

Chapter 15 – Love Will Conquer

It was warm that Wednesday evening. Adam and Hannah still had their bedroom window open as Adam eased into bed. Cody lay calmly at the foot of the mattress and peered over at Hannah as she walked into the room, wearing her regular cotton pajamas and rubbing lotion into her hands, the citrusy fragrance quickly pervading the room. She gracefully sat, cross legged near Adam's head, and watched Adam intently as she continued rubbing lotion into her hands. Adam lay calmly on his back, reading.

"Do you think Justin and Erin will hit it off?" Hannah softly asked.

"No," Adam said curtly before chuckling. "Do you?"

"Nah. He'll be alright though."

"Yeah, yeah."

"I wish we could help," Hannah mumbled, "but I don't know what else we could do."

Adam placed his bookmark, closed the book, and held it against his hip. "I was thinking about it some today, and one thing is clear to me." Adam cleared his throat. "Justin's not looking for perfect ten, ...like you." Hannah lightly smacked him. "No, I mean Erin's beautiful and sexy and all, but that's not the kind of girl he's looking for." Adam rolled over on his side, facing Hannah with his elbow on the bed and resting his head on his hand. "He's seeking that one in a million in regards to all the other less superficial qualities. He wants someone who's agreeable, around the clock, someone who's smart and engaged, someone who's open-minded and understands all the basics of life and can look at any situation and quickly assess, for themselves, what's going on."

"Well," Hannah said as she relaxed her hands on her lap, "when he finds her, I hope she realizes how lucky she is."

"Hannah," Adam said, chuckling, "he'll get inside her head. With his scrupulous attention to details, he will so soon have so much insight into her and understand what makes her tick even better than she. He will have all her hopes and dreams figured out and be able to explain them better than she could explain them herself."

"And," Hannah added, "I suspect he will do everything he can to see that her dreams are realized, even the ones that don't involve him."

Adam smiled and asked, "Do you have any dreams that don't involve me?"

"Well, you're indirectly involved, but sure, there are things I want to do with my life before I'm gone, and of course, I will want your support and want you by my side, but yes, some of my dreams are my deal." Adam narrowed his eyes as he stared at her. "Oh, don't worry," Hannah said. Even though her hand was still slightly clammy from the lotion, she reached over and gently ran her fingers through his hair. "Those dreams are secondary to our dreams." Hannah leaned down and kissed him gently. "Hey," she said, pulling her head back, "we should still stop by and help Justin with his date tomorrow night."

Adam nodded. He reached over and set his book on the nightstand. "You know what else?" Hannah raised her eyebrows. "I think Justin needs to exercise more. That's key. He would feel so much better and be so much more confident. He would sleep better."

"He would look better," Hannah interjected. "Girls can be superficial too. Are you and Josh still going to invite him on hikes?" Adam shrugged, and Cody raised his head as soon as he heard the word hike. Hannah watched Cody for a couple seconds before he slowly lowered his head again. "Justin could also eat a bit healthier too," she added, continuing to watch Cody.

"It would have a huge impact on his image and his presence, wherever he goes."

"Kelsey may have helped him even more than we know. We'll see, but I think he'll be fine."

"You know what else I thought about this morning after we left the coffee shop?" Hannah looked at him and tilted her head as he said, "Justin and Kelsey are night and day, right?" Hannah raised her eyebrows and nodded playfully. "If Justin and Kelsey can get together and help each other out, Republicans and Democrats should be able to get together and help each other out too." Hannah rolled her eyes and chuckled. "No, listen to me," Adam said enthusiastically, "the situation really is symbolic. I do see it as an example of how two different parties, stuck in completely different places, can come together and do absolute wonders for each other and for the greater good of both."

"Your grand plan?"

"Yes. By getting together and talking, they could help each other appreciate a great new place they could get to …together, through compromise."

"Your grand plan?"

"Yes, it would be such a wonderful new place for both parties and for everyone involved."

Hannah got up and strolled to the bathroom. Adam lay back and closed his eyes. As Hannah returned, she turned out the lights and slowly slid into bed, nuzzling up to him. Cody let out a soft whimper and rolled to his side.

In the pitch black, Adam softly asked, "Did you see Josh's response when he learned you were pregnant?"

"Yes."

"What the hell?"

"Oh Adam, he just doesn't want to lose you."

Adam scoffed. "Are you suggesting that he has some tacit, legitimate, selfish reason to not be happy for us?"

"He knows that once we have a baby, it's going to be different and that scares him."

"It won't be that different."

"Hah," Hannah interrupted. "Adam, it will be different." Adam let out a deep sigh. "Don't worry, he's happy for us."

"It won't be that different. We're not moving to another planet. We're not going through some sort of metamorphosis. We'll still be doing the same stuff all the time, going on bike rides and watching football." Hannah smiled and patted Adam on the chest as he added, "I wonder if his response is more related to Emily than us."

"How so?"

"Maybe he's worried about being totally alone with her. I'm sorry, but I'm not sure she's into it. She seems to be yearning for something more." Hannah nuzzled up closer to him. "She loves that the gallery's turned out to be a lucrative endeavor, but she sure seems like she's merely biding time until a better opportunity comes along. I think he's really trying too, but she's not responding to the effort."

"Well, they're buying a house together now."

"Exactly. She's excited about the house, but I worry she might be into it because it's a distraction from the reality of being with him or at least because it helps her to feel more comfortable about being with him. What do you think she's bargaining for?" Adam hesitated as he waited for a response, but Hannah was silent. "I know she wants to have kids," Adam went on, "but I'm still not sure she wants to do it with him." Adam tilted his head toward Hannah. "I trust you'll do everything you can to help."

"What do you expect me to do?"

Adam rolled over and pushed Hannah on her back. He slid to the other side of her and faced her as he lay. "Do you understand what you did for Kelsey?"

"Adam, you should credit Justin, and it was your idea to get them talking."

"No, no. You saved her. There's no way Justin or I could have talked to her. You were the key connection to getting it started and getting her to gain some proper perspective."

"Well, we'll see," Hannah groaned. "I will always worry that Drew may be right, that's she's just a ticking time bomb and it's only a matter of time before the bomb goes off."

"No, no," Adam said tersely as he rested his head on her shoulder. "She'll be fine. She's fine now." Adam kissed her on the chin. "You don't have to worry about anything anymore. There is no way Kyle's going to let anything happen to her. I really believe he'll manage to respectfully and delicately keep her from making another bad decision. He'll be watching over her, every day." Adam suddenly put his left hand on his forehead and gasped. "Oh my gosh."

"What?" Hannah asked, rotating her head toward him. The darkness notwithstanding, she could see the whites of his eyes.

"You saved Kyle too."

"What?" Hannah blurted out, startling Cody.

"I'm just now realizing this."

"Adam, stop it."

"No, listen, among all this, you cracked that nut, Justin." Hannah chuckled and shook her head. "Second, you saved Kelsey. But who knows what would have happened to Kyle had we lost Kelsey. I mean, I guess he would have been fine if she never learned he loved her, but what if we lost her? I don't know what he would have done. Maybe he would have blamed himself."

"You're thinking way too much."

Adam sighed. He raised his head and snuggled up to her. "Hannah, I would kill a dragon for you."

Hannah playfully said, "Well you can't just say that. I'm sorry, but you have to prove it. I won't believe you until you actually kill a dragon for me."

Adam raised up on his elbow and shook his head. He slowly pulled back the covers. Hannah tried to pull the covers back up, but Adam held the covers down over her legs. She conceded and peered up at him. Their pupils were now fully dilated and she could see the silhouette of his head against the soft evening light on the wall. He pulled her pajama top up over her belly and looked down at her. As he began caressing her tummy, he ran his hand around in a circle. He sniffled.

"Adam?"

"Oh Hannah," he said, his breath hitching as he began to weep. "You're going to be such a good mother."

"Adam?"

"Sadie was right. You proved it this past couple weeks. You're going to be so loving and so caring and so nurturing. You really don't see the influence you've had over Kelsey? You saved her," Hannah scoffed. "Our little baby is going to have it so good with you as their best friend in the whole wide world." Adam quickly wiped his eyes. "You don't even know how happy I am that you're going to be the mother of this child." He leaned down and kissed her belly. "I love you so much."

"Hey, come here," she replied softly. Adam slowly lowered his head. He rested his head against her shoulder, and as Hannah managed to wrapped both her arms around him, he continued slowly circling his hand on her belly.

"Who am I without you?" she whispered.

Adam wrapped his arms around her. "This is all I want any more. Hannah, I don't look forward to anything anymore. I just want time to stand still, right now." They lay still, holding each other, for several minutes and fell asleep in each other's arms.

THE END

About the Author
Craig Boroughs resides in Summit County, Colorado and encourages everyone to help expand the awareness about the science, rudimentary details, and completed evaluations of all issues that affect our communities, the country, and the world and demand that the basic facts behind every situation be considered by policymakers, and between your efforts and your work, go read, love for love's sake, and vote!

9 780692 863077